All about Training the Family Dog

Also by John Cree

TRAINING THE GERMAN SHEPHERD DOG (ALSATIAN)
NOSEWORK FOR DOGS

All about Training the Family Dog

JOHN CREE

PELHAM BOOKS

First published in Great Britain by
PELHAM BOOKS LTD
44 Bedford Square
London, WC1B 3DU
1984

British Library Cataloguing in Publication Data

Cree, John
  All about training the family dog.
  Dogs—Training
  I. Title
636.7′083   SF431

ISBN 0 7207 1529 6

Phototypeset by Sunrise Setting, Torquay,
and printed and bound by
Butler & Tanner Ltd, Frome

To my daughters
Frances and Joyce
another generation but with a similar interest

Contents

List of Illustrations

All photographs were taken by John and Irene Cree with the exception of the one on page 108 which was taken by David Ireland for the *Fife Free Press* and we wish to thank both for permission to publish.

Photographs

Acknowledgments

Quite a number of dog owners in both the domestic and the competitive fields have unconsciously supplied much of the material for this book, a good deal of which has been collected by the observation and study of humans with regard to their reactions to canine activities — in the home, in the street, in the park or during organised training sessions.

To be more specific, I must acknowledge with thanks the help received from owners who attend the Ardfern training sessions — those owners with problems and those who have overcome such troubles but wish to advance their knowledge and training techniques. Their co-operation in the setting up and photographing of situations to illustrate the various important features is much appreciated.

I wish also to thank David Ireland for his photographic assistance and practical advice regarding my photography, and Irene, my wife, for her critical assessment of this work and the many hours she spent typing the manuscript.

Part I — The Principles

1 A Dog in Your Home

Your dog is one of the family, a companion and source of enjoyment, but he can also be an embarrassment, infuriating, and can cause great displeasure to yourself, your neighbours or complete strangers by the unpleasant situations which develop through his activities.

His companionship and the pleasure he gives must outweigh the periodic irritations of his wayward activities otherwise he could not remain a tolerated member of the household — but is this good enough? His misdemeanours may be small and infrequent and this may be due to your own understanding and ability. On the other hand you may not have a natural gift for understanding your pet's requirements and could well find your dog's companionship rather trying.

In many ways we can liken dogs to children; remember, children can be as exasperating and the source of as much displeasure as any dog. Despite the wealth of experience we have accumulated on bringing up children and educating them to become independent and responsible, we still make many mistakes and misjudgments. No wonder we have so many problems with our domestic pets.

Canine psychology is a specialised subject but a layman's understanding of its principles will be quite sufficient for our purpose. Canine actions and responses are the heart of our subject and will be dealt with in the simplest of terms and in sufficient depth to achieve the desired objective of control over our canine companions in usual domestic situations.

The problems the dog owner has to face can be many and varied: his dog's failure to come back when called; a determination to pull on the lead; destructive escapades; aggressiveness to others (both human and canine); possessiveness with a bone, food or a favourite toy. These are but a few of the problems which must be avoided or corrected at an early stage.

The dog

The social behaviour and the ease or difficulty with which you achieve the requirements for the domestic scene are greatly affected by your choice of canine companion. Some dogs are much more responsive than others, falling into the pattern of home life without the need to consider any formal methods of training. In cases like this, dog and owner have been matched to perfection: the dog has inherited a very balanced character whilst the owner, by design or accident, has the knowledge and ability to prevent unsociable activities from developing. However, such combinations are rare.

A Cocker Spaniel.

It must be recognised from the start that no two dogs are of the same character, temperament and inherited instincts; even within a single litter of puppies there are variations. Some puppies are bold and brash whilst others are rather shy and retiring. Quick-witted puppies will size up situations as they are developing; others do not seem to notice such changing conditions.

The various working qualities which have been bred into different breeds add another factor to the composition of each dog. Gundogs will show quite a different set of charactertistics to those from terrier families, and even within the gundog group each breed has been developed for its own special contribution to the sport.

A Hovawart.

A Wire Fox Terrier.

A Golden Retriever
puppy.

The difference between one dog and another manifests itself in many ways; some dogs can be naturally attentive whilst others show quite a streak of independence; some are very attached to their own kind whilst others prefer human companionship; some are very energetic and enjoy plenty of space to run free whilst others have a much lazier outlook on life; some are very inquisitive and will stop to investigate anything which takes their fancy whilst others can seem to spend their time day-dreaming; some are very protective and will warn off strangers whilst others show no sense of discrimination and will even welcome burglars into their homes. However, all dogs will have a certain mixture of all these characteristics bred into their systems and in such varying strengths that each dog can be considered as unique.

It should also be recognised that dogs reach mental maturity at different ages. The toy breeds seem to mature, both mentally and physically, at an early age. Border Collies can be ready for advanced training whilst they are still classed as puppies. However, Boxers, Dobermans and such like require much more time to settle down before accepting a responsible role in life. The period of immaturity certainly affects the time any youngster takes to adapt to a sociable domestic existence and any prospective dog owner should bear this in mind.

Due consideration should also be given to your dog's inherited characteristics and this can be extended to cross-breeds and mongrels for they too will inherit the characteristics of their parents. This may result in some excellent combinations and produce youngsters of very sound character and temperament; on the other hand some genetic combinations will produce dogs which require a great deal of understanding if they are to have any chance of fitting into the domestic environment.

The owner

The character, temperament and understanding of the dog's owner will have a great deal of influence on his pet's behaviour. Successful dog owners can be compared with parents who succeed in bringing up well-behaved and considerate children. To achieve such ends parents require to have their children's interests at heart, being prepared to spend a good deal of time in helping to guide them into the future whilst setting a good example by their own attitude and consideration. At the same time, they have to be prepared to act firmly and fairly to counter any deviation from the accepted path. These basic principles apply to the training and development required to bring out the best in your canine companion, which objective is the aim of this book.

As dogs vary considerably in character, temperament and inherited instincts, so it is with humans who also vary in a similar manner. Shortness of temper, impatience and lack of consideration towards your dog will cause the animal to experience a fair measure of distrust. Situations can develop where he will not be able to interpret your requirements nor will he be able to understand your changing moods. On the other hand indecisiveness or over-tolerance will encourage the dog to take advantage. This results in canine disobedience with the dog taking the initiative of the pack leader.

Some owners take a dominating, overbearing or ruthless approach to try and ensure that their dogs give an immediate response to their requirements, only to find that the relationship has lost its pleasures — for both parties. Yet other owners will treat their dogs as human beings giving them the credit of a full understanding of the human mind as well as the human language, with the result that their dogs obey certain instructions but fail to understand others.

In order to overcome such problems the dog owner must assess his own failings and try to obtain a reasonable balance of patience and decisiveness, of understanding and consideration as well as learning the strengths and weaknesses within the character of his dog.

The partnership

For you to enjoy your dog's company to the full he must be well behaved, have a bit of spirit — to enjoy his life under his master's roof, and be considered a member of the family — but in his proper place.

A dog is a pack animal by nature; he is either the pack leader or just a member of the pack findng his own place in the pecking order. Within the family he can only be a member of the pack and his place in the pecking order must be below the other members of the family. If he is brought up correctly, treated fairly with consideration, and encouraged to enjoy his life he will understand his place in the community, just as nature intended.

Although the dog owner must be the pack leader the relationship can be treated more as a partnership, with the dog as the junior and man as the senior member of the association.

It must be recognised, however, that dogs know their owners better than the owners know their dogs — or themselves. Dogs seem to be capable of analysing all our strengths and weaknesses — they have much more time than we have to carry out this analysis.

The true loyalty of a dog to his owner has got to be earned. The goodwill which is built up between them can be likened to a bank balance, with the dog's loyalty being measured in a similar manner to that of a bank manager to a client. A bank manager's loyalty is built up on confidence and any overdraft is granted on his assessment of the client's ability to honour his debts.

The expectation of loyalty from a dog is based on goodwill being the currency the dog understands. To go too deep into debt without the dog feeling that the situation will improve will certainly damage any loyalty already built up and, therefore, do great harm to the partnership.

2 Human versus Canine Logic

It is important that we, as dog owners, think about our own actions and reactions as well as considering a dog's approach to life.

It is rather unfortunate that when dealing with a puppy human actions are often unconsciously geared to those of raising a family. The actions of dogs and children can be alike in so many ways, especially young children at the toddler stage who are not yet able to express themselves verbally.

We all like to play with children. A small child loves a game of chase, with Mum or Dad pretending to run at great speed until finally catching up with the little one. As the toddler grows and at some stage runs away at the wrong moment, down a busy street or in a shopping precinct, he can still be caught and gradually taught that there are times for fun and games and times to behave.

When the language barrier has been broken and a toddler begins to speak and to understand what is said to him, he will learn *why* he must not run away and also understand the warnings or threats if he continues to misbehave.

Let us look at the same situation with a puppy. Puppies love games as much as children do; pups will chase each other and so will grown dogs as they continue with the fun of the chase in adult life. If puppy owners take the place of litter mates and chase their young puppies in fun, where does it stop? Very young puppies are easily caught but in a matter of weeks they can outstrip their human elders or hide in corners which are quite inaccessible. When a puppy begins to feel a measure of independence and refuses to come when called, then serious chasing begins with the puppy enjoying the game but the owner becoming more frustrated and bad tempered because of the pup's 'disobedience'.

As the puppy grows up and continues with greater skill to avoid capture the final outcome is punishment at the hands of his owner and usually as the result of a fit of temper. No wonder dogs do not understand human logic.

The foregoing is only one example of a situation where people apply to canine mischievousness human thinking which is based on the experience of child behaviour.

I think it is true to say that a young child who has not yet learnt to speak is probably on a similar mental plane to our domestic canine companions. Once a child has learnt to speak, the form of communication alters and the understanding between child and adult reaches a level which could never be attained between dog and owner. The communication between a dog and his owner, because of the language barrier, always remains at a lower level. Nevertheless it can still reach a very sophisticated stage of perfection with practice and experience.

A child who can communicate can understand praise and punishment. He can be warned of the consequence of any failure on his part to behave or to obey. He understands delayed punishment — being sent to bed early when Dad has discovered some misdemeanour which occurred earlier in the day. This, a dog does not understand.

To try and explain to a dog that he is going to be punished if he does wrong, or to punish him after the event, is not only a waste of time but destroys the confidence he has in his owner. He cannot understand what is happening and will only become confused.

A dog's level of understanding is based on what is pleasant and what is unpleasant, and on what causes the pleasant or unpleasant situation. The words praise and punishment are not in his vocabulary. For instance, if a dog gets an ear nipped in the tailgate of a car as it is being closed, the pain and unpleasantness of the situation sticks in his memory and he will keep clear of it in the future. The dog cannot be warned that he is likely to get his ear nipped and be expected to understand the reason for your warning. If he is spoken to in a manner which keeps him well away from the tailgate he will stay there because he has been commanded to, and the possible tailgate injury does not affect his reasoning to obey.

A wasp sting will bring out a variety of reactions the next time a dog hears a wasp. Some dogs will show respect and keep clear, others will show fear and hide, whilst still others will show aggression and will probably get stung again for their efforts; they may even be stung time and time again, but will feel the satisfaction of having disposed of a buzzing pain carrier. What is certain is that the dog will react each time he realises a wasp is close enough to cause unpleasantness.

Canine logic will make the dog react to *his* interpretation of the cause of the pleasant or unpleasant situation.

3 A Background to Training

Dog training is a form of education where firstly, by means of this book or any other book on the subject or by attending training classes, owners are educated on how to train their dogs. It is only when the owner has a grasp of the subject that dog training can progress.

As novice owners themselves are learning whilst they teach their dogs, it will be seen that many dogs receive their education second hand. Every transfer of information, from book or trainer to owner and then on to the dog, is likely to cause a misinterpretation of the original intention. With the dog at the end of the line he is most likely to be condemned as the stupid link in the chain and may well be blamed for the failures which originate from the source of instructions or the owner.

We, as human beings, require an incentive or inducement to learn. Children at school, students at college or adults at work are all being educated or trained in a particular skill. If the incentive is strong enough, or if the goal is well worth achieving, we will work hard enough for it. The subject will attract and keep our interest and any obstacles will be overcome because we appreciate the value of success; we shall also realise the meaning of failure.

Fear as an inducement to work affects humans and dogs in a similar manner. Attention is split between the subject being taught and the cause of the fear. There is no doubt that dogs can be and are trained through fear of their owner but it does show a lack of ability to achieve the objective by more constructive and considerate means.

Fortunately, as humans, we can visualise the end product and will work for it. With dogs, the end product is much more immediate and if it cannot be visualised the dog will go its own way. A dog will normally act in a manner which he thinks is in *his* best interest.

Communicating with your dog

A dog cannot be expected to obey an instruction he does not understand. To understand and act on an instruction a dog must be able to translate his owner's requirement. The instructions may be verbal or visual, or even a combination of both, and when the dog has translated these instructions he will act in response to canine logic.

A hand signal is quite useless if the dog does not see it.

To illustrate the problems of a language barrier consider the meeting of two people of different nationalities, each without knowledge of the other's language. The visual actions of hands, arms, facial expressions and body movements will become the principal means of communication. The meaning of any verbal utterance can only be of value if the visual expression is properly understood. Any misinterpretation of personal movements or facial expressions will give the verbal utterance a wrong meaning and this will undoubtedly create a very confused situation.

Even without the problem of a language barrier, misunderstandings between two colleagues, friends or relatives are commonplace. How often is there a variety of interpretations from a dicussion or even a simple instruction.

If it can be acknowledged that human beings are often far from perfect in communicating from one to another it will be recognised that a great deal of thought must be given to the art of communicating with a dog. Dogs learn through repetition and consistency and this is where patience and consideration are very valued attributes in a dog owner. The dog should not be blamed for any failure to understand, but any such failure should result in a reappraisal of the approach to communication.

Sign language and physical assistance are very important aspects of dog training, especially in the earlier stages of instruction. If a dog is being taught to sit when instructed, it is useless just to *tell* him to sit until he knows and understands the meaning of the word. He should be enticed to put himself into the sitting position or physically assisted to sit. At this stage, no verbal instructions are necessary, for he will soon know from the actions of his owner that he is expected to sit. It is only when he responds in accordance to visual instructions that the verbal instruction to 'sit' will be of value. The visual and physical actions become signals with a meaning and it is only when the dog reacts to those signals that verbal instruction can have any effect.

Our every movement or utterance tells a dog something, but he will only pick out the actions which are meaningful to him. Unintentional communications are most obvious when his meals are being prepared or when the 'old man' puts on his shoes for the final walk of the evening. The dog may appear to be asleep but activities of this nature will communicate his master's intentions and he will react accordingly.

Dogs are often credited with the ability to read the thoughts of their owners, but this ability to anticipate is probably due to the fact that a dog can string together the activities of his owner where an unconscious word or action alerts him to the sequence which is likely to follow. The time of day also triggers off the expectation of certain activities which are of value to him.

The evenings of every work day find my dogs alert to the sound of my car. Many other vehicles pass at this time but only my own car sets off a reaction. I very occasionally come home at lunch time, but when this happens I am generally in the house before they realise I have come home. Their reactions are conditioned to the appropriate time of day for my return — they are not expecting me to arrive at mid-day and so do not distinguish the sound of my car from any other as they do in the evening.

4 Principles of Control

To achieve the measure of control which is necessary for normal domestic purposes we should consider the various features which require particular attention to ensure that your dog will respond to and respect your requirements. It would therefore seem timely to consider the most common and frustrating problem experienced by a great number of dog owners. This is the recall — getting your dog to come back to you when you call him. This single, but indispensable, requirement from a dog brings out the essential principles of control.

The ease or difficulty in achieving a recall can make canine companionship a pleasure or a misery. Most dog owners who turn to training classes for help have done so because their dogs will not come back to them when called. This, I find, is the biggest headache and a problem which varies from one situation to another. I have heard it said so often, 'Sometimes he comes back immediately he is called, but if there is another dog around there is just no hope of getting him back. I can shout and shout but he will just ignore me.'

Unfortunately this type of situation is very common and many dog owners require guidance to prevent or combat such indications of canine defiance as and when they occur. Providing a dog understands what is wanted, any failure to respond can usually be taken as defiance and, strictly speaking, this is perfectly true, so what is the explanation for such behaviour?

Conflict of interests

If you call your dog and it so happens that there is nothing of interest taking his attention, then he will come to you. On the other hand he may be gnawing away at a lovely new bone, or he may be giving his attention to an amorous bitch. Under these conditions failure can be assured unless the ground has been well prepared to exert your authority on his reluctance to obey. There is a tremendous conflict of interests.

The principal requirement then is that of getting your dog's attention for nothing of value can be achieved without it. The foundation of good control, of prompt obedience to your instructions, is based on the ability to obtain your dog's attention as and when you require it, to retain it and then to make good use of the situation you have created.

With a strong conflict of interests the pointed finger was insufficient to gain Zula's attention.

Distance is another very important feature which affects your control. If your dog is relatively close he is less likely to defy you, and conversely the greater the distance which separates you the more defiant he is likely to become.

Distance, however, does bring another factor to bear on your dog's reaction. Many dogs become worried if the distance between themselves and their owners becomes too great. Their interest changes through a sense of insecurity and thus begins to coincide with that of their owners.

If we now put these two factors together — the conflict of interests and the distance between yourself and your dog — you should fully understand the reason why your dog appears to be inconsistent in his response.

Gaining your dog's attention

Good and constructive dog handling is based on the dog owner's ability to change the interests which cause canine defiance, or to recognise that his measure of control is not good enough under the prevailing circumstances and to act accordingly.

For instance, take a situation where the dog is in the garden and refuses to come into the house when called. This act of defiance, or lack of control, must be countered. A simple remedy would be to make a pretence of preparing his meal — this will probably bring him in (unless he has just been fed). It would, of course, be unkind not to reward him for his response and a titbit along with some praise will serve the purpose. Any failure to give him a reward would soon make him realise that he was being conned.

I well remember a professional animal photographer who was taking some photographs of my two German Shepherds for publicity purposes. He used a whole series of tricks to gain the dogs' attention for each shot.

A tit-bit being appreciated by Fritz for sitting promptly.

A little tap on the camera lens holder with his finger nail brought instant attention. The 'miaouw' of a cat, the words 'pussy cat', the deep growl of another dog — all brought positive results, but each trick lost its appeal after the second try. Those dogs were no fools and the lack of anything of interest meant changing to a new ruse, but this professional had quite a repertoire.

To a dog, your use of his name can only mean that you are talking to *him*. Your tone of voice and the volume applied can tell him almost everything he wants to know about your attitude of mind. His name is therefore the prime attention getter and as his owner it is your responsibility to use it in the manner that will be most effective. You should assess his likely reaction before deciding on the tone and volume you will apply, varying it to suit the occasion. As a back-up for getting his attention, any other suitable noise can be employed at the same instant as you call his name. Clap your hands or stamp your foot, for instance. All such actions can be effective.

What follows the use of your dog's name is completely dependent on the situation. You may use a hard and uncompromising tone of voice to get his attention, but to follow up with a command in the same manner is likely to destroy the effect. Any harshness of voice used to gain the dog's attention has served its purpose and must be followed by a softer tone of voice and encouraging actions to attract the dog to you. If your dog happens to be sniffing at something some twenty paces away, a positive and urgent use of his name will be required to get his attention. To follow through with a stern command to come to you will certainly result in canine apprehension and the chance of a favourable response very unlikely. To follow the call of his name with an urgent but exciting invitation to come to you, thereby giving him the knowledge that it will be well worth his while, will make his interest coincide with your own.

Although you may use your dog's name sharply to gain his attention there are seldom occasions when it is necessary to shout. Dogs, like children, become immune to continual shouting or nagging and if a dog owner is continually doing so then there is nothing in reserve for the occasion when full volume is really necessary.

Praise and punishment

I have already said that the words PRAISE and PUNISHMENT are not included in the canine vocabulary and, as such, a dog understands neither. He does, however, understand what is pleasant and what is unpleasant and will relate these feelings to his *immediate* situation, not to what happened five hours earlier, or five minutes or even five seconds ago. If you come home and find that your favourite slipper or one of your best gloves is chewed to pieces there is no value in smacking your dog or giving him the sharp edge of your tongue. He will associate your displeasure with the welcome he gave you, and any recurrence will only convince him that welcoming you home makes life unpleasant for him.

If you catch your dog in the middle of doing something wrong (say digging in the garden), give him a short vocal blast, but make a fuss of him the moment he responds; he will then understand that digging causes unpleasant reactions. If you follow up your rebuke by immediately calling him to you with the anticipation of fun, a titbit or just some affection, you will soon make him understand that the recall brings pleasure.

Throughout this book I shall make great use of the words PRAISE and

REWARD because in our minds they can only mean pleasantness. PUNISH-MENT is too drastic a word and can be taken too literally, therefore I prefer to avoid its use.

Use of natural situations

Although there are many different techniques in dog training much can be achieved through the use of natural situations. In fact a very observant and dedicated owner can achieve excellent results just by avoiding the major pitfalls and by making use of natural training situations which are not even noticed by most people.

By this, I mean the natural association of a word of instruction with the action which the dog is performing of his own volition. When your dog goes to sit of his own accord, ask him to do so whilst he is in the act. When your dog is about to lie down, encourage him with 'Good boy, *down* you go', said softly with the emphasis on *down*. When he is coming back to you of his own accord, for whatever reason, make full use of this voluntary return to call him in with the fullest possible enthusiasm.

With some dogs this type of training is quite sufficient for the domestic scene, but with others the natural approach can be used to supplement instructive training.

Canine attentiveness

As already stated, attentiveness is based on interest. Any form of study or training is best terminated whilst the student is full of interest. A lecturer who can capture the attention of his audience will certainly achieve the success he deserves. Similarly, the dog owner must have a real interest in learning how to train his dog and the dog must be equally enthusiastic and receptive so that he gives his full attention to his owner. Obviously if the owner does not have full commitment to his dog during a training session then partial success is the best he can expect. Both owners and dogs will concentrate on learning only so long as the training is interesting. This statement may well be disputed by the 'hard men' in canine training circles, but their methods frequently result in dogs with broken spirit.

It will be recognised that young puppies cannot be expected to remain attentive for lengthy periods, neither can older dogs who have never been given any previous training and are not used to paying attention for even short periods. The question is, how long is a short period and how short is a long period? I suppose it is about the same as the 'length of a piece of string'.

I find the best way to assess possible periods of attentiveness is to consider your own ability and what motivates you. When the interest is strong we can all be attentive for lengthy periods. Watch a cricket match and see how a batsman can dig in for hours, until with one lapse of his concentration he is out. A tracking dog will follow the scent of his quarry for miles and at an average speed of two or three miles per hour — quite a spell of concentrated attention.

Now take the man in the street, how long does he apply his attentiveness to a subject which does not take his full interest? Think about it and ask the same question about his dog.

In dog training, enthusiasm, especially when generated from the owner, will certainly help to prolong periods of attention from the dog, with each step within the particular session being terminated before boredom catches up with either the owner or his dog.

Commands

Within dog training circles any instructions to a dog are defined as commands. Even the Kennel Club Regulations covering competitive obedience, in the UK or any other English-speaking country, detail all such instructions as commands.

The word command can be defined and interpreted in various ways, one dictionary definition being 'to exercise supreme authority over'. This interpretation, if applied by any dog owner, is certain to create an undesirable response from his dog and a rather unrewarding companionship. However, if the interpretation is 'to influence', the dog will certainly recognise this as a much more pleasant approach.

'Command', like 'punishment', is a rather harsh expression and is likely to be interpreted as such. I shall therefore in this book employ the expression 'instruct' and make minimal use of the word command. Our approach to training will thus be one of enthusiastic participation and cooperation on the part of both owner and dog.

Again within dog training circles it is accepted that all commands be given in a single word and preferably one of a single syllable such as 'Sit' — 'Down' — 'Come' — 'Heel'. One cannot argue against this principle; it is just the same as learning a foreign language — single words help to keep it simple. However, there are other considerations.

Single short words tend to come out as uncompromising commands. The more they are used the less appreciative is the owner of the unsympathetic approach he is applying.

I often listen to people who have been attending dog training classes and hear them continually snap 'Heel — heel —heel' at their dogs as they drag them along. I have also watched them as they shout 'Come' in the most uncompromising manner when their dogs are showing a mild interest in something which has taken their attention.

In both these cases words of encouragement along with the emphatic operative instruction would be much more appropriate. '*Ben* — come on, son, *heel* — that's a good boy' with the appropriate physical assistance is one approach for walking to heel. For the recall: '*Ben* — that's a good boy — *Come* on, son, in you come.' In both these examples 'Ben' is the attention getter with 'heel' and 'come' as the key words, which are uttered in softer encouraging tones as a verbal inducement designed to influence the dog's reaction.

This does not mean that a refusal to obey should be accepted but a balanced approach should be attained in order to achieve a happy responsive dog.

Kim knows her place and will walk just as nicely down the High Street.

Problems — prevention or cure

There is no doubt that the prevention of a problem is of much more value than trying to effect a cure, but often the problem is upon us before we realise that it has been allowed to develop.

Problems which have become established in a dog's behaviour are likely to remain evident for the rest of his life unless something is done to counter the situation. Do not bank on them disappearing of their own accord. You may think that your dog is going through a phase, but such phases usually become habit forming and will last a lifetime. It is therefore very important to understand and remember that *a canine action once repeated can well be the basis of a habit.* If that action is to your benefit — cultivate it. If not, make sure that it is stopped before the habit has formed.

A puppy should never be encouraged to jump up on chairs; such behaviour will quickly develop into a habit which can be quite undesirable when he is a full-grown dog. Again, a pup should not be allowed to jump up at his owner as a form of welcome — a habit which will be regretted when muddy paws leave their mark on a nice clean suit or dress.

Some owners think it amusing to hear a puppy growl when they try to take away his bone, only to discover later on that no one dare go near the dog whilst he is enjoying the pleasures of a marrow bone.

Most problems generate from puppyhood or the dog's adolescence, but they can arise from particular situations in which the dog finds himself. Your dog may be of a very balanced character and well behaved until your neighbours acquire a cat. From then on, your flower beds may never be the same again; the dog who previously never put a foot wrong may now show no respect for boundaries.

Without your being aware of it, some mischievous schoolboy may tease your dog through the garden fence. This can be the instigation of barking sessions every time inoffensive little boys walk past your gate.

I wonder how many dogs have been teased in this manner without the owner knowing about it.

Such problems cannot be readily anticipated, but when they do become evident steps should be taken to avoid a recurrence. There are times when a cure must be sought, but there are other occasions when it is easier and more prudent to avoid the situation and thereby prevent it from happening again.

Take, for example, the kitchen bin raker. A dog which is left in the kitchen on his own whilst his mistress goes shopping may never think of pushing his nose into the rubbish bin until one day when some meat wrapping is put into the bin near the top. Boredom and a sensitive nose reveal an interesting find which results in a deeper investigation until the kitchen is littered with rubbish.

All dogs learn very quickly when it is to their advantage, so a habit will form if no one is present to catch the dog in the act and promptly deal with the situation. There is only one solution in a case like this: simply remove the rubbish bin each time the dog is left on his own, thus eliminating the temptation. Prevention is much easier than trying to devise a cure.

The approach to training for the avoidance or correction of the various problems which are discussed in this book will be based initially on general control and prevention of those problems from developing. The approach to countering problems which have already taken a firm hold is another important aspect which will be fully dealt with.

Prevention will be mainly directed to puppies although the techniques are generally applicable to dogs of all ages. The cure or correction of problems is often based on the techniques for prevention and as such both aspects are treated in each phase of training.

Collars and leads

The choice of a collar and lead for your dog plays a significant part in your own ability to apply control over your pet. However, its measure of control is more dependent on how this equipment is applied than on the equipment itself.

Firstly, the principles of lead control should be fully understood in order to appreciate the value of selecting the most suitable type of collar and lead.

The collar and lead have three functions:

(1) As an indispensable aid to training. To enable you to have your dog walk by your side, to come when called, to sit, to stay and as an aid in many of the situations which require corrective training.
(2) As a form of control when you realise that without them you do not have sufficient influence for the situations present or anticipated.
(3) As a form of influencing your dog's activities when you do not wish, or

are not in a position, to give him your full attention. Out for a walk where traffic can be a hazard is an ideal example of this requirement. In fact a dog should always be on a lead whilst he is off his own premises unless you are in an area where supervised freedom can be given.

The type of collar and lead should be selected with control training in mind, but of course the equipment is ideally suited to everyday use as a certain amount of training of a preventive or corrective nature can be required at any time.

Collars: At this point it would seem appropriate to mention that *by law* a dog, when away from its own premises, should wear a collar bearing a name and address tab for identification purposes.

There are two basic types of collar which are in common use and they are made from a variety of materials.

(1) The check collar (sometimes called the slip collar, or more commonly known as the choke chain) is probably the most effective collar designed for general purpose dog training. The original intention of this type of collar must have been to choke a dog into submission, hence the more common name of choke chain. However, an enlightened approach is now being made with its application and its purpose is to *check* a dog's action so that the desired response can be obtained.

With a properly fitting check collar a short but sharp jerk on the lead is all that is required to gain the dog's attention and guide him into the situation you have in mind.

The standard check collar is a chain composed of metal links with a ring at each end. It is important that this collar is put on the dog in the correct manner. With the dog at your left side, the collar is worn in such a way that it will automatically slacken off when the tension is released.

The correct size of collar for a dog is one which will go over his head with a little to spare. A check collar bought to fit a puppy will obviously have a limited life and some allowance should therefore be made for growth. Conversely an over-long check collar round a dog's neck can easily fall off and get lost, or a dangerous situation can arise should the chain be caught up with the result that the dog chokes.

Another point to remember is that a check chain will cut away at the hairs round the dog's neck when under tension, with small-link chains doing the most damage. Many owners are concerned about this, especially with show dogs, and prefer to use check collars made from nylon or leather which are quite satisfactory.

The best check collar I have seen was given to me by the late Olive Point from the Dogwood Obedience Training Classes Inc., Richmond, Virginia, USA. This is a round nylon type which is too short to go over the dog's head; it is clipped round the animal's neck and can then be used in the same manner as the full-link check chain. The slightest jerk on the lead is immediately felt by the dog and its proper use ensures an instant response. Unfortunately, these collars are not available in the UK at the time of writing.

Another variation of the full slip check collar is the type which is adjustable and has a limited slip. This is an excellent collar both for training and for general purposes. It is normally called a combi-collar and is usually made from webbing with a short loop chain which creates the tightening effect when pulled.

(2) The buckle type of collar is generally made from leather but there are now types made from nylon or cotton webbing. Others, especially for small dogs, are made of cord all-in-one with the lead. Although the combined lead–collars are not strictly classed as buckle type they do come into the same category of non-slip collar. This non-slip type of collar has little value as an aid to controlling a dog unless in the hands of an expert, but when adjusted correctly it can be considered adequate as a permanent attachment round a dog's neck to carry the identification disc.

Kapra and Klan in their combi-collars and a single lead.

Leads: There are three main factors to be considered when purchasing a lead, viz:

(1) The length of the lead.
(2) The material of which it is made.
(3) The type of clip and attachment.

(1) The length of the lead should be such that you have room to manoeuvre. The standard four-feet lead is a suitable length for general training and domestic control. A shorter lead does not give you any scope to develop satisfactory techniques for control and should be avoided.

Longer leads do have their value. I have a seven-foot lead which I find to be particularly useful in the early stages of training but it is rather long for general use and is likely to create handling problems for the novice owner.

(2) Good leather leads which are well softened are certainly worth having. To me they feel good to handle and that, I think, is their principal recommendation. A poor quality leather lead will not last, especially when a big strong dog has to be brought under control.

Nylon webbing leads have become very popular and are a good reasonably priced substitute for leather, especially those with a soft woven double thickness of nylon webbing where there is no hard edge which can cause discomfort to the dog owner's hands.

Chain-type leads with a leather grip are, to my mind, the worst type of lead to buy and the discomfort to the owner in using this lead for canine control prevents its proper application.

I usually find that owners who use chain leads do so because their dogs insist on chewing a leather lead. This is a bad habit which should never have been allowed to develop in the first place. Details for corrective training will be given in the section on loose lead walking.

(3) The quality of the clip and its attachment to the lead is very important. Unfortunately some lead manufacturers seem to give little consideration to this factor and it becomes the weak link in the dog handler's means of control. Before purchasing a lead you should ensure that the clip is fitted with a strong attachment.

The type of clip itself is now a matter of fancy. The scissor type seems to have a good record but I feel that it is too easily opened and a dog can be released unintentionally.

The trigger type of clip has now become the most popular and I think its strength and designed safety has earned it its popularity.

Although the type of collar and lead to be used is your personal choice, the result of your selection can be a help or a hindrance in your efforts to obtain satisfactory control of and prompt attention from your dog.

Part II — The Training

5 The First Steps in Training

All the training procedures which follow give full consideration to the requirements of young puppies straight from the litter to mature adults who have not had the advantage of a properly controlled upbringing.

The ground rules are described for preventive training through to the curing of major chronic problems. With young puppies, juniors going through a period of adolescence or older dogs, the principle is the same, but with young puppies the correct approach will ensure that many of the techniques will not be required. Older dogs who have already become a problem should be taken right through each stage of the training procedure applicable to the fault in question.

The moment a puppy comes into the home, training begins by teaching him to adapt his toilet requirements to suit his new environment. After a very short settling-in period (this may be as little as twenty-four hours) he considers himself to be one of the family. It is at this stage when little acts of destruction often come to the fore.

The basis of our educational approach will come out in the handling of both these problems.

Toilet requirements

Our starting point is the arrival of your puppy in his new home.

So far his toilet needs have been satisfied by stopping and doing his business wherever he wanted. During the first few weeks of his life his place of convenience would more often than not be in the nest, or his bed, which will usually be the whelping box. With his Mum there to clean up after him he did not have a care in the world but, as his world grew in magnitude, the area outside the nest would take his attention when he woke up after each of his many rest periods and more often than not he would do the needful after stretching his little legs and this would take him out of his bed.

The little fellow would soon learn with his developing mind that to be caught short would mean a wet or messy bed to sleep in and would in future make a point of controlling his toilet needs for that few seconds needed to tumble out of his bed and then relieve himself.

At this stage it must be appreciated that a young puppy's toilet requirements are tuned to sleeping and eating. Whenever he wakes up, the accumulation of waste during the preceding rest period requires to be disposed of; similarly, after a meal the intake of food generates a progression of activity throughout his system which again results in the need to dispose of waste matter.

We, therefore, find that puppies will generally attend to their toilet requirements immediately after sleeping and eating, with the area just outside their bed becoming the area of convenience.

When the pup reaches the age of some eight weeks he is taken from the only home he has known and transferred to a completely new and domestic situation.

His house training now begins. The kitchen floor, or the lounge carpet, or any area to which he has access becomes his toilet area; your small puppy knows no different — habit and custom have created the situation.

A new routine must be formed to replace the existing toilet habits. To do this you must recognise his time of need and create the situation where he will do his toilet in the area *you* nominate. This requires vigilance on your part, to ensure that you are prepared to act as soon as he wakes and gets out of his bed. Never wake a puppy to suit your own timing — his system is unlikely to be in tune with your requirements and puppies, like babies, are much more contented if left to wake in their own time.

Make sure you are ready to act as soon as the pup has finished a meal. Whether the dish is empty or not act as soon as he has decided that he has eaten enough.

We now come to the first principles of dog training — that of gaining your puppy's attention and getting him to follow you to his new toilet area.

We shall assume that this is in the garden, and to start with the region nearest to the door should be considered as satisfactory. In these early days the shorter the distance over which you are required to keep your puppy's attention the better — and your aim is to get him there, on his four little legs, as soon as possible. If circumstances make the distance to the new toilet area too great, then it will be necessary to pick him up and take him out for the first week or so.

Getting and keeping your puppy's attention is the name of the game. Remember, your objective is to get him outside as quickly as possible. Your voice and actions should be the main inducement, but if you require an additional incentive then use one. This could be a rubber bone or a squeaky toy on the end of a piece of string and dragged in front of the puppy as you entice him to the door. Your voice and actions, however, are most important. Call him as you walk backwards, 'Ben — come on, son — that's a good boy — come on, Ben', and keep this up with all the feeling that is necessary until you get him out to the toilet area. You must not lose his attention for a second. Let the rest of the family know that there must not be any distractions during this period.

If you have another dog do not let him distract the puppy from your objective; in fact, if you can concentrate on calling the older dog the puppy may want to follow and this could be the inducement you require.

When you get the pup outside give him a little praise, or if you have used a toy as the inducement let him have it to play with. You now blend into the background — say nothing, and do nothing to take his attention. An attempt to encourage him to do his business would be a waste of time and may well inhibit him, delaying the action you require. Remember that at this early stage he has no way of knowing what he is being encouraged to do.

If the weather is inclement or if there is a good programme on TV there is a temptation to try and hurry him along. *Do not try it.* If you have used a play article to get him outside you will find that he will quickly tire of it if nobody is going to play with him. The boredom due to the lack of activity will let his mind turn to the purpose of his visit. If he is not desperate, just give him time and nature will take its course. If you have used an older dog to induce the puppy to come out, the two may play for a short time but the puppy will stop when he is ready to perform.

Wait and watch him the whole time, and as soon as you see him starting to do the needful, praise him and use the expression which will eventually let him know what you want him to do. The words you use are your choice but it can go like this — *'Clean* boy, Ben — you are a nice *clean* boy.'

Eventually you will be able to induce the required reaction by saying 'Come on, Ben, be a *clean* boy' repeated as required, but make sure the habit is well formed before you start *asking* him to do his business.

The area of your original choice may well be too near the house and you may eventually prefer to have a more permanent convenience area at the far end of the garden. You will find the change easier to achieve if you cover his little pools with earth. The saturated earth can then be scooped on to a shovel and deposited in the area of your choice. You can also put little bundles on to the shovel and treat them in the same manner.

When you can entice your pup to the new area his smell will be very evident to him and this should encourage an easy change-over.

Daytime 'accidents' in the house are liable to happen, but every accident is going to encourage the next. It must be kept in mind that scolding or punishment is of no value and you must consider it to be your own fault for not being sufficiently observant.

'Accidents' during the night are likely to go on for some time. A baby in nappies is not expected to be dry in the morning — so don't expect too much from your puppy. If there is only one pool on the floor in the morning it probably happened when he woke up to the noise of movement in the house — so if you wish to avert that 'accident' forget about your day clothes and your own needs and get down to the pup before he is sufficiently awake to think about activating his own disposal unit.

As mentioned above, one 'accident' in itself will encourage the next. The smell, faint though it may be, after the puddle or mess has been cleaned up, will attract a puppy back to the same spot. A good strong disinfectant is therefore essential to minimise this source of temptation.

I remember one youngster of mine who was very clean and we were proud of our puppy-training results until one evening I went through to the hall without shoes only to find that I had one wet foot after stepping onto a nice thick woolly rug situated there. When we lifted this rug to clean it we discovered that this was the fourth such accident in almost the same area. The rug was cleaned then put away until this youngster was more reliable. Replacing the rug a few weeks later brought out no new lapses in his toilet habits.

Success depends on your dedication, with failure requiring unrestrained devotion.

Preventing acts of destruction

A puppy is never knowingly naughty or purposely destructive. Although this is a point which may be open to argument, we base our training on the premise that any puppy is only doing what is natural to him.

He may chew the edge of the carpet or the leg of a chair as a result of teething problems or just plain boredom, or a combination of both. His chosen article may be one of Dad's slippers or a sock where the comforter with his master's scent on it may have been the initial attraction.

Teething, boredom or even a mischievous outlook in the puppy's make-up are the main causes of these destructive episodes in the little fellow's life. There are three main requirements which must be appreciated if destruction, lost tempers and unwarranted punishment are to be avoided.

(1) Plenty of toys of his own.
(2) An attentive household.
(3) A tidy household.

We will now take these requirements and examine the reasoning behind them.

(1) PLENTY OF TOYS OF HIS OWN: Most young children have a multitude of toys; some are rarely looked at, whilst others seem to get daily attention. The most prized possessions are usually the inexpensive and scruffiest things imaginable. Children also get bored with their toys unless some adult is prepared to spend some time with them playing with these toys.

A cardboard box of toys may be good enough for some dogs but a 'higher class' of dog enjoys a basket.

Young puppies are the same; an old sock or an old cardigan can give a great deal of pleasure and, at the same time, these items can take a lot of punishment before they finally disintegrate into small pieces. The traditional hard ball or rubber ring which can be rolled across the floor can bring out the instinct to chase and will also give pleasure when the family are prepared to participate.

Have a toy box for your puppy. All his bits and pieces can be put into it when they are not required. One or two old bones, the remains of an old slipper, a ball and a rubber ring and anything else which has taken his fancy.

With the right encouragement he will act like a child and will pull out every toy until he reaches the one he wants — this will invariably be at the bottom of the box.

A cardboard box from the grocer is good enough and is likely to last much longer than one would expect. I had one such cardboard toy box for a youngster; it was emptied every day by this pup and it lasted through adolescence — a whole year's use before it was thrown out.

(2) AN ATTENTIVE HOUSEHOLD: At any time during a puppy's waking hours he is liable to get up to some sort of mischief and when left to his own devices he may well look for some new interest — washing which is drying on a clothes horse may take his interest. Until he has been taught to leave such things alone, vigilance is required to ensure that such destructive excursions are avoided.

A puppy owner must develop a suspicious mind and if all is quiet he should be thinking 'What's that pup up to now?' — then go and find out.

(3) A TIDY HOUSEHOLD: I am afraid this means more than having everything in its place. Dad's slippers may look neat and tidy sitting by the fireside waiting for him to come home after a hard day's work but they are a great temptation for an active puppy. Putting them away in the bedroom does not help very much either if the doors are left open so that the puppy can investigate that wonderful extension to his normal environment.

Anything which can be carried, pulled or chewed may be considered as fair game to a puppy — minimise the opportunities by keeping as much as possible out of reach until he has been trained to ignore the items you consider to be taboo.

This 'squeezy' bottle could have been the shoe.

A destructive pup with the cheapest toy of her own.

Now we can look at constructive training — and this brings in the important factor of gaining your puppy's attention at any instant.

Whenever you catch your puppy giving his attention to some prohibited item call his name — sharply and with meaning, although there is no need to shout with such volume that the neighbours are aware of the event.

What you do next depends on his likely reaction.

(a) If you expect him to stay where he is or to run away, take no further action but wait; if he decides to leave the forbidden item, praise him from a distance: 'That's a good boy, Ben.' If he goes back to the item then use a verbal stopper before he gets started — '*Ben, no*' should stop him — and again praise him from a distance. Again wait to see his reaction; he will probably realise that you really mean business, but if he thinks otherwise and returns towards his forbidden prize repeat the process with a great demonstration of your disapproval and indignation, but from a distance. One movement towards him may lay the foundation for fear and the temptation to run away from you — avoid this situation at all costs. So long as your voice and distant actions can prevent your puppy from continuing with the destructive episode, you are winning. If you can then entice him to play with one of his own toys and have fun with you, he will not consider you to be nasty and responsible for spoiling his fun but will begin to realise that the forbidden item which was so attractive is now the source of much unpleasantness.

(b) If you expect him to come back to you when you have disturbed him call him and give him something of his own to play with. Play with him for a very short period, ten to fifteen seconds is quite long enough, then leave him to play on his own. Sit down and pretend not to be watching but observe his actions and if he makes for the forbidden item, stop him short by calling his name with a firm '*Ben, no,* come on, son, where's your ball?' Immediately go back to playing with him for another very short spell, then again wait and watch. If necessary keep repeating the process until he realises that he cannot play with the forbidden item.

As your puppy's scent from the saliva in his mouth is now on this forbidden item it may well be a temptation for future exploits in moments of boredom. A wipe with a cloth wrung out in disinfectant may act as a suitable deterrent.

To catch the pup thinking about a forbidden chew is the ideal situation for building up the knowledge in his mind that he cannot chew to his own fancy. To catch him in the middle of such an act certainly gives the opportunity to retrieve the situation. *But* to find out after the event means a complete and total failure in this instance; harsh words or punishment after the event are of no value and will only leave the little puppy with the feeling that he has a very unjust and unpredictable master. The only chance of retrieving anything from the event is the knowledge that your puppy is likely to repeat it and you can then be on your guard to prevent the next attempt.

Remember — an attentive and orderly household can be most effective in preparing a young puppy for a well-behaved period of adolescence.

Although the foregoing paragraphs have dealt with basic puppy training, the principles hold good for an adult dog with similar problems.

Your own approach in the past may well affect his reactions to your enlightened attitude but this should not prevent you from persevering towards a more sociable existence. It takes time to undo the damage which has caused your present problems before real progress can be made.

Food stealing

The stealing of food can be classed as a variation of canine destructiveness although the temptation can be much greater. Food must, therefore, be considered as fair game for any puppy, or older dog for that matter, until he understands that taking such items is taboo. Some dogs never seem to learn and the same can be said about many households where temptation is left on a low table or such like.

Mac is caught in the act of stealing food.

The degree of care which is required is wholly dependent on the dog's past history as well as the natural inclinations of a greedy dog. A very greedy dog may well be rather difficult to cure, attentiveness and tidiness being the only answer. However, the food stealer must be countered with the full approach already described for curing the destructive dog.

Food stealing may well be mistaken for destructiveness when one finds the contents of the kitchen pedal bin scattered over the floor, when all the dog was after was the paper in which had been wrapped a pound of prime steak. This could be quite a temptation for any dog and to avoid a recurrence you will need to take the steps described on page 42.

Lonely puppies

Puppies who are left at home unattended for many hours can be a problem, especially if the family are out working all day. The problems can still occur when arrangements are made for somebody to look in at lunchtime to make sure everything is all right. Such conditions are a breeding ground for problems and too often lonely puppies become problem adult dogs.

Household items are destroyed, little pools saturate the rugs and carpets or little smelly bundles create an unpleasant homecoming.

Crying, howling and dogs barking for attention can also be caused through loneliness. None of these problems should be blamed on the puppy; it is not his fault that he is locked up for lengthy periods and deprived of attention.

Canine boredom, uncontrolled exuberance and the needs of nature play their part in the regrets at buying a puppy in the first place. There is no simple answer for these particular problems; there is no way that a puppy can be trained to comply with normal household requirements without the guiding hand of an understanding owner. It is surprising, however, that so many puppies survive this period and settle to become well-behaved adults without that helping hand.

The problems related to crying, howling or barking dogs can, in the main, be prevented or cured. Lap dogs probably find solitude hardest to accept and it is important to understand that an excessive amount of personal contact and petting can make short spells of loneliness a misery instead of an acceptable part of life.

With prevention or cure as the objective to having your puppy or adult dog accept his own company and not to be continually looking for yours, a start should be made by putting his bed in the kitchen or some other suitable place where he can have peace and quietness on his own for an hour or two. At a time when he is tired, especially after a play period or a long and enjoyable walk, leave him in the selected room on his own with a nice juicy marrow bone or an appetising hard biscuit in his bed. A well-used marrow bone can be filled with mince and the concentrated effort in trying to get into the middle has made many a dog forget his loneliness. If it is feeding time leave him to enjoy his meal alone.

When your dog is prepared to accept a couple of hours without your company, spent in relative quietness in the house, he can probably be left on his own whilst you have an hour's shopping expedition.

Lengthy periods of loneliness can be accepted by a dog who has been brought up to accept shorter spells of his own company.

Any other solution to the problem of the lonely dog is second best. It may be arranged that a kindly friend or relative can pay a visit, give the youngster a walk and then leave him to sleep off his tiredness. A sheltered kennel and run may be an answer, especially if shared with a canine companion. However, there are times when the problems of one dog are doubled with two.

A pet pen can be used to contain a youngster during the absence of the family, but this does not really counter the misery of such a life. It will only ensure that domestic destruction has come to an end. Chapter 16, however, gives fuller accounts of pet pens and their uses.

6 The Control You Must Achieve

To have your dog come back to you when called or to ask him to carry out any other function you must be in a position to control the situation.

The ability to control your dog's actions is very much dependent on your own understanding and appreciation of the principles which have been discussed in the earlier chapters. Success is also dependent on your skills in applying these principles and methods. Basic control, therefore, is built on your ability to gain your dog's attention and get him to come to you when he is called. Without that measure of control one of two different types of situation is likely to develop.

(1) Your dog will become a nuisance to everybody. Hours can be spent in trying to get him back, or even to find him. Whilst he is being defiant and is out of your sight anything can happen — he could be chasing a farmer's cattle or sheep, he could be teaming up with other strays. I say 'other' strays because under these conditions your dog is also a stray, even if it is only for a short period. He may well find his way home but during this period of freedom his actions will be based on primitive canine instincts, the instincts and actions of a stray dog.

He could be a danger to himself and to others; an accident may end his life or the life of some unsuspecting motorist. A dog which does not come back when called is an embarrassment to his owner and he has in fact taken over as pack leader.

(2) To prevent such an embarrassing situation many owners do not let their dogs off the lead whilst they are out of the garden. Every walk with the dog, short or long, through streets or in the country is a restriction at the end of the lead. No fun with a ball or a stick, no pleasant excursions into the undergrowth and absolutely no feeling of freedom.

Under either of these conditions — why keep a dog? In short no owner or dog can obtain real enjoyment out of their companionship under these conditions.

To come when called

The objective is to obtain your dog's attention in any situation, or at any distance, with an immediate response to your call when he will happily return to you.

The important factors which should be utilised to achieve your objective can be listed as follows:

(a) Using your voice in a manner which guarantees that he will pay attention when you call his name.
(b) Changing the tone of your voice to ensure that your dog will respond to your call to come.
(c) The application of body and hand movements along with verbal encouragement whilst your dog is coming back to you.

The use of your dog's name is the means of getting his attention — the call of his name must mean something to him — and you can also take advantage of his curiosity. When he is walking away from you with nothing special on his mind give him a little tap with a finger on his hindquarters as you call his name.

This tap on his hindquarters will cause your dog to turn his head to see what you want and the use of his name will create the association between name and the desired attention when he happens to be further away from you. His attention will be with you for that second — make use of it — call him in to you and make a great fuss of him. Your tone of voice will change from a sharp *'Ben'* to a gentler and more persuasive 'Come in, son, in you come, that's a good boy.' By this time your dog, or puppy, will be with you and will be enjoying the pleasure of your attention. You can have a toy handy with which to play with him or a juicy little titbit as a reward.

There are many occasions when a natural situation lends itself to a call. If your dog is coming towards you of his own accord, call him in, but remember that his attention is already with you and there is no need for any sharpness in your voice as you call his name. The gentle but expressive 'Ben, come in, son, in you come' is all that is required.

Feeding time is another occasion when the call to come can be applied with great effect, especially with puppies. Older dogs know the routine around feeding time and one seldom has the opportunity to call them — they are usually waiting with great expectancy.

Avoid calling your dog when his attention is on something else unless you are convinced that he will respond. Do not, in the early stages, create a conflict of interests. It is preferable to go up to your dog, give him a little tap on his hindquarters with your finger as you call his name thereby taking his attention away from the interesting distraction. Having gained his attention in this manner you can then move backwards and encourage him to follow you.

Again it is the correct use of your voice along with encouraging hand and body movements which draw your dog to you. Treat your dog as you would a small child; get down to his level with outstretched arms and encourage him to you, but draw your arms back as he converges on you so that he can get close to your body for praise and affection.

Kapra on recall with a kneeling owner giving maximum encouragement.

Remember that the distance between yourself and your dog affects the control you have over him. The closer he is, the more responsive he is likely to be; the further away he is, the more defiant he can become if he does not wish to come to you. With some dogs, however (as stated earlier), a greater distance can give them a sense of insecurity. Such a dog will be more than happy to come to you when he realises that his human companion is not at hand to give support. Dogs who react in this manner are easily trained by your creating a greater distance between the two of you whilst calling in an urgent tone of voice as you run away from him.

I have already mentioned that, in the early stages of training, you should not create a conflict of interests between your own requirements and your dog's desire. As you gain more control with a happy regular response to your call, situations can be selected where there is a mild conflict of interests when deciding to call him from a distance.

Do not call him from his favourite bone or his dinner dish, but select a time when he seems to be mildly interested in a smell on the ground or when he is just going his own way for no obvious purpose.

Judge the situations when you can expect success — where the distance is not too great and the canine interest is moderate. Failure to achieve the response you are expecting shows an error of judgment on your part rather than an act of deliberate defiance on the part of the dog.

Puppy games help to establish habits, both bad and good. Puppies love to be chased and this game can be the foundation of apparent defiance in the future, also the source of many other problems. This has already been discussed in Chapter 2.

However, if we reverse the roles, puppies also like to chase. If you run away, especially from a very young puppy, he will be only too happy to chase and enjoy some little reward for catching you. Affection, praise, a titbit or a toy to play with, it does not matter which, so long as your pet gets real pleasure out of it.

This type of enjoyment does not need to be restricted to young puppies and games of this nature can also help to overcome problems of defiance with older dogs. Unfortunately, children tend to treat their canine pets like other children. They will chase and they like to be chased, with puppies and dogs treating children as their own kind. This should not do a great deal of harm unless the children are allowed to take their pets out into the open where the dogs can eventually become pack leaders and start to defy their immature owners.

An owner playing 'hide and seek' with an inattentive dog.

The worried dog has found her owner. This is much better than a worried owner looking for the dog.

Games of hide and seek are probably the best means of attaining an attentive relationship with any dog, especially an impressionable puppy. This can be done with great gusto where your dog sees you disappear into a wood, behind a fence or the corner of a building whilst you encourage him to find you. Remember the roles are never reversed so you have to look for him.

Quite often when out walking with my own dogs, at any age, I hide behind a tree, then wait and watch for their reactions when they discover that I am missing. As they learn the game so young, and they know how to use their scenting powers, I am found in seconds. Sometimes I lie down in the long grass and it is only when they pick up my scent in the wind that they know where I am. Games like this create attentiveness and a foundation for the recall.

Problems related to the recall have many sources. Some breeds have a very strong desire for freedom and may respond very well as puppies but maturity can bring independence and defiance to the fore unless it is firmly discouraged. Unintentional acts of encouragement to defy have caused many an owner a headache (these situations have already been discussed). A threatening attitude on the part of the owner has made many a dog frightened to come back when called.

To give a wayward dog a hiding on his eventual return is probably the most negative approach which could be applied and will destroy any confidence a dog has in his owner. The dog will soon learn to dodge the intended blow (just like any little boy when Mum or Dad decides that such a measure is necessary) and he will soon learn to keep out of reach, then not to come back at all.

Little boys and dogs learn very quickly to dodge a swinging hand - or a newspaper.

A dart forward to grab a pup will soon result in an 'artful dodger'.

There is the owner who will make a grab for his dog when it comes within arm's length — until the dog with his reasoning and greater agility learns to dodge the grasping hand which means capture and a period of detention on the end of the lead.

The effects of an uncompromising or thoughtless owner's attitude will bring out obvious canine reactions to such conditions. Some dogs will completely ignore the owner's shouts, his commands and the final appeals to his dog to return. Others will think that it is a continuation of a great game and may even run up to the owner to within arm's length then dart away. Yet others will just stand and watch, and when the owner takes one step forward the dog is away and making sure that a safe distance is maintained.

Remember that any unpleasantness on the dog's return will be associated with the act of returning and he will be still more reluctant to come back in the future.

The secret of a good instant response to your call is to make sure that you are always in a position to ensure that your dog will come back to you. If you expect him to defy you or if he is not at a stage of understanding your requirements you should move yourself into a position where success is guaranteed, or wait for the correct moment before acting.

To achieve a better understanding with your dog, special training sessions are advisable. You can start in the house if you wish, or possibly the garden. Open spaces away from home should also be used for training sessions.

The first part of this section dealt with the conditioning stage of gaining control of your dog: how to achieve the attentive dog with the will to come back when called. Now you will want to consolidate that approach or to start correcting the dog with wayward tendencies.

Make use of a slip collar and a good lead of reasonable length. The standard four-foot lead is satisfactory; you can use a longer lead if you wish but one shorter than four feet will certainly be of little value.

Now take your dog on the lead and let him go where he wishes. If he pulls just let him; if he stops to sniff at something allow him to do so. Do not apply any control, let him do what he wants.

When you are ready, call his name as you give a sharp tug on the lead. Move backwards and away from him as you call him with great urgency and enthusiasm. You want your dog to come to you — so create a real desire to do just that. Any firmness in your voice should only be the use of his name to obtain the instant attention which is so necessary, but this must be followed immediately by the enthusiastic and encouraging call to come.

Good timing with a sensible application of the lead and slip collar will have a remarkable effect, even on the most defiant of dogs. However, the wayward or defiant dog will take time to become fully responsive to the call on its own.

As you become more confident you can make use of stronger distractions. It is only when your dog responds to the call of his name without a tug on the lead, under more severe conditions, that you can think of progressing.

A very responsive dog can now be given a measure of freedom but he must act with responsibility when you call, but do give consideration to distance and the nature of any distraction. Remember that the greater the clash of interests the less chance there is of a satisfactory response. Create success and avoid failures.

Some dogs with a warped sense of responsibility, which may well be the owner's fault, require an extension of the lead training using a long line. Owners may feel that the use of the long line in training is degrading for a dog when in fact they are really more embarrassed at their own apparent failure. What other people think about this apparent failure to control a dog doesn't matter — it is the eventual success which is important.

The 'apparent failure' which necessitates long line training may well be due to inadequate handling on the part of the owner, but it is quite often due to a very defiant and self-willed dog.

Fritz being controlled at the end of a long line.

Fritz being permitted to chat up a girl friend, but still under control from a distance.

Wellington learns to come when called via the long line.

A line of about twenty feet in length should be quite sufficient although a longer line of some thirty to forty feet may be more in keeping with the requirements of the fast-moving and excitable type of dog. A strong nylon cord with a clip tied on the end should suit the purpose. Good nylon cord of sufficient weight to suit your dog can be purchased from most hardware stores or sports shops. A clip of the type which is normally attached to a dog's lead can usually be obtained from the local pet shop.

The application of the long line, which should be attached to the slip collar, is identical to that of the lead. Allow your dog plenty of freedom and the opportunity to do what he wants. If necessary, move away from him to ensure that there is a reasonable distance between yourself and your dog. Do not pull on the line at this stage but if he wishes to pull you just follow at his will. Allow him to take an interest in something of his own choice. Then call him by name and get his attention. *Do not* accept a negative response; any failure to give you his attention must result in a positive and immediate action on your part. Call his name again with extra firmness and at the same time give a sharp tug on the line. Immediately change the tone of your voice to one of enthusiastic encouragement and urgency and use any physical movements which will ensure that he comes back to you quickly. If necessary move backwards at speed to draw him to you the quicker. Never move towards your dog when you call him. At best this move will slow him down and at worst he will run away.

Never pull your dog in to you on the line. This will achieve nothing of value and will only cause fear which will make your dog even more reluctant to come back to you in the future.

Do not forget to praise your dog for coming back; make it worth his while. Do not be too ready to discard the long line; if necessary let your dog drag it round behind him when you are out for a walk.

There are some dogs who will come back right away when called but will run past their owners full of exuberance. To these dogs it is all a game but to the owners it can be frustration at its limit. The correct use of the long line and the voice as the dog reaches the limit of the line will have a very sharp and memorable effect. His feelings will be hurt and all the sympathy he can get will soon make him realise that it is much more pleasant to make a dignified return.

Make sure he responds every time you call him in and if you have to take hold of the line at any stage this is evidence that you are not ready yet to discard it.

Only ten consecutive successes will give you confidence in the result of the eleventh. Any indication of a return to his wayward attitude will necessitate a return to the long line.

Never be reluctant to go back to an earlier stage of training.

7 Loose Lead Walking

Loose lead walking is obviously a very important ingredient in the relationship between a dog and his owner.

A dog who pulls his owner to their destination creates a situation where the dog has taken over full control and where the owner has abdicated his authority to that of the dog. This is one of the most common problems in dog ownership and, like the failure to come when called, owners have difficulty in understanding why it occurs and what to do about it.

Although the dog who perpetually forges ahead is the most common offender, the dog who stops at every post or lamp standard, or who dawdles along in his own time, can also be classed as an unsatisfactory loose lead walker and needs corrective instruction.

To make an outing a pleasure Barney must learn to walk nicely on a loose lead.

Barney has taken control and stops at his own 'convenience'.

If we again start by considering the puppy stage in the dog's development, it can be demonstrated how these problems can be prevented in the first place. The earlier a puppy becomes accustomed to a collar and lead the better as much can be done to prepare him for loose lead walking in the period before he is clear of his injections and permitted to explore the outside world.

The various types of collar available have already been discussed. If it is preferred that the puppy should wear a collar at all times this should be of the buckle type where it can be adjusted to a size which will not allow it to be pulled over the puppy's head, or alternatively a combi-collar which has been suitably adjusted. The loose type of check collar, which may be ideal for training, is not suitable for general wear as it can easily catch on a projection and could well be the cause of a very unpleasant experience for the pup; at worst he could be strangled.

The initial training can be carried out with the buckle-type collar, a check chain or a combi-collar. A lightweight puppy lead will also be required, although the very early stages can be completed with a light piece of cord attached to the collar.

Firstly, your puppy must become accustomed to wearing a collar before any attempt is made to use a lead. Twenty-four hours should normally be long enough but an extra day or two should be allowed for the more sensitive pup. There is no hurry.

Having his collar put on or having the lead clipped to the collar should be considered by your puppy as an event which results in pleasure, but initially you can not expect him to think ahead for that pleasure. It is only when the chain of events becomes established in his mind that he will appreciate the value of his collar and lead.

Until this sequence is understood your puppy (or older dog) should experience immediate pleasure when the collar is fitted or slipped over his head, by means of praise and possibly a titbit with the praise.

When you feel that your pup is ready you can attach the lead or a length of cord to his collar and let him drag it around for a short spell; five minutes at a time is quite sufficient and this exercise can be carried out three or four times a day if you wish.

Whilst he is allowed to drag the lead around, either in the house or the garden, he must be watched to ensure that it does not snag on anything or, if it does, you are in a position to release him immediately thus avoiding any unpleasant associations during this breaking-in period. Two or three days of this sort of conditioning will probably be sufficient.

The principles applied in the recall training now come to the fore. Have the little fellow drag his lead around whilst in the house or garden then position yourself so that you can surreptitiously take hold of the end of the lead, i.e. whilst his attention is elsewhere. Give a little tug on the lead, just sufficient to get his attention; call his name and drop the lead at the same time then immediately call him to you encouragingly. As with the recall training apply your voice in the most suitable manner, 'Ben — come on, son, in you come,' and again make his response worthwhile.

You can now let him go and repeat the process as before. The number of repetitions of this procedure during one training session depends on your puppy's reaction, probably three to six times will be sufficient.

At this stage make no attempt to carry the end of the lead but watch his reaction during each short training session. Your puppy will soon learn that when you pick up the end of the lead he is going to be called in. If his attention is with you when you pick up the end of the lead (or as a result of that action) there is no need for the tug or the sharp 'Ben'; modify your approach to 'Ben — come on, son, in you come.' With this type of encouraging reaction from your puppy you can keep hold of the lead as he comes in to you.

Perseverance with this programme of training will ensure that as soon as you pick up the end of the lead your puppy will react by coming to you — but never take this for granted, remember to make it worth his while with a little praise.

Having progressed this far, now is the time to start getting him to walk with you for a few paces. Hold the end of the lead but use encouragement rather than the lead to keep him with you. The temptation of a titbit in your hand or one of his toys will always help to keep his attention.

If you have to keep tugging the lead there is something the matter, there may be too many distractions and he cannot concentrate on you if there are more interesting activities in his vicinity. It is possible that you could be trying to progress at too fast a pace and basing your progress on too weak a foundation.

Traditionally your dog should walk at your left side, although this is not so important for the domestic dog owner. It is, however, standard practice for handling dogs in various forms of competitive work. Therefore to avoid any confusion it is recommended that you follow the standard practice and the training sequences which will be described relate to a dog walking at your left side.

The correct fitting of the check chain, but demonstrated with the left wrist instead of using the dog's neck.

The incorrect fitting of the check chain; it will not slacken when tension is released.

When a check collar is used, remember that there is *only one correct way* to fit it and it is most important that it is thus worn at all times. Assuming that your puppy is to be taught to walk at your left side, the fitting of the check collar is as illustrated. When fitted in this manner a slight tug will tighten the collar and a relaxing of the tension will allow the release. To help ensure that the check collar is being fitted correctly you can experiment by fitting it to your left wrist, giving a pull and release to illustrate the resulting action.

By the time your puppy is clear of his injections he will be ready for his first real sight of the outside world. Choose a time when it is quiet, or take him in the car to a quiet spot — the fewer the distractions the better. All the new smells in this wonderful world may prove to create sufficient distractions in themselves.

Having put him on the lead, give him a few minutes to investigate these new smells then give him a little tug as you call his name, with the request to come '*Ben* — come on, son, in you come,' and get him to come in to you. When you are happy that he will respond, encourage him to walk with you for a little distance; again your puppy's progress will depend on his reaction.

Avoid any situation where he will try to pull you; if he is determined to pull then change your direction and give him a little tug with encouragement to follow. Again it is '*Ben* — come on, son, are you coming with me?' If he is not happy with the change in direction, stop and apply the recall procedure, but keep moving backwards in the direction you choose to take. With praise and encouragement try walking again, but revert to the recall whenever he objects. Do not overdo the loose lead walking but build up gradually.

Eventually your voice should be sufficient to attract his attention whenever he pulls ahead or lags behind because of some interesting distractions.

Training for loose lead walking must be carried out every time your dog is taken out on the lead for a walk. Remember that whenever he is on the lead you are consolidating the faults or virtues of your loose lead handling.

Loose lead walking with your dog should be like walking with a human companion. You are not actually watching each other but are conscious of the other's movements; to stay together one person must respond to the speed and directional changes of the other. With a dog, however, it is you who determines the pace and the direction in which you travel. Your dog must be conscious of your movements and alert to any of the directional changes you might make.

The early training sessions and any periods of retraining are quite strict and many movements are carried out in order to make your dog very conscious of your presence. You may make a sudden change of pace or direction to ensure that your dog is continually monitoring his position. We, therefore, return to the recall training procedure described on page 49.

With your dog on the lead call his name to gain his attention and, if necessary, give a short tug on the lead. Use great urgency and enthusiasm as you move backwards calling him in to you. As he reaches you turn and walk away as you encourage him to walk by your left side. Walk for just a few paces then stop and give him some praise, along with a titbit if you are using food as an inducement. You can also make a game of it unless you have a very excitable dog. Temper your approach to suit your dog's character.

The owner's backward movement also encourages a fast recall.

Each time you call your dog in to your side use the recall approach, but as soon as you start walking with him by your side (with his head just about level with your side) use the phrase '*Heel*, Ben, that's a good boy.' Walk for a dozen or so paces each time before stopping to give him some praise.

The expression you use as your dog comes to heel is not particularly important and it may well be similar to the recall, 'Come on, son, in you come.' Your dog will automatically associate your requirements with your actions. I find it rather disconcerting to hear dog owners out in the street shouting '*Heel, heel, heel,*' continuously with their dogs not paying the least attention. It is much more important that your dog comprehends your movements and actions; this understanding of visual aids will come much more quickly than any words of command.

With loose lead walking it should be borne in mind that you cannot expect your dog to keep his attention on you *all* the time, just waiting for a change of speed or direction. A word of warning that a change is imminent will be much appreciated by your canine friend.

The problem dog

The training details which have just been given are general to loose lead walking but special measures are often required for the persistent and dedicated canine delinquent, the problem dog who has not had the benefit of correct training from the start. This is not the dog's fault and little if any blame can be levelled at the owner. What we have to do now is look for the basic cause.

I would liken this problem to that of a child learning to read. Parents normally lay the foundation at home by helping their children with suitable books and other visual aids. The parents are able to pass on their own knowledge because they were well taught in the first instance.

Dog owners are not always so fortunate. Some learn by observation, others have a natural bent for dog handling. However, most owners require to be taught, to have the cause of the problem explained, and the techniques of prevention or correction demonstrated.

Many of the puppy training techniques can be applied or adapted to the needs of older dogs who have acquired undesirable habits, but in most of these cases a much firmer attitude must be applied.

The major problems can be classified as follows:

(1) The dog who forges ahead at the end of the lead.
(2) The dog who lags behind.
(3) The dog who stops and sniffs at every opportunity.

(1) The dog who forges ahead and has his owner trailing at the end of the lead is probably the biggest problem and he needs very strong and unpleasant measures to control his enthusiasm. A few of the various corrective measures are suggested here.

(a) Stop dead in your tracks and at the same second give an almighty tug on the lead as you call him to heel. A three-second vocal blasting will probably do a lot of good, but you should immediately follow this up with praise. When you give the almighty corrective tug on the lead you may find that a backward step will give added power to your action. Do not worry if you pull your dog off his feet, a somersault or two may make him realise the unpleasantness of his own actions. It may look unkind, but this form of treatment will cause no physical harm. A dog's neck muscles are such that injury will be restricted to his feelings; the indignity resulting from your action will have him looking for sympathy. Do not disappoint him — your solicitousness will help to shift the blame on to himself. When you continue your walk the interjection of a stern warning now and again with a follow-up of praise will help to remind your dog of the unpleasantness caused by his own forceful actions.

This kind of exercise will soon prove the strength of your lead. When I am helping to correct wayward dogs for owners who cannot grasp the significance of positive action, I always examine their leads very closely before commencing. In the past I have broken a number of poorly designed leads (not my own) which goes to show that it is wisest to purchase the best quality.

I would mention here that some inconsiderate handlers tend to put the check collar right up to the base of the ears. This is a very dangerous practice and can easily cause injury. On no account should a forceful tug be applied with the collar in that position. The collar placed halfway up the neck should be satisfactory.

(b) Every time your dog thinks of forging ahead you should cross his path by making a sharp left turn so that he will bump into you and will have to give way to your change of direction. Call him in to your side as you continue walking then praise him for doing so, and whilst his attention is with you, carry out a few more sharp left turns with praise on completion of each turn.

(c) Tight anti-clockwise circles of about ten to twelve feet diameter and walked at a smart pace will ensure that your dog cannot forge ahead of you. This approach may not be practical in the earliest stages but it is certainly a good conditioner when your dog begins to understand the reason behind the sharp tug which brings him back into line.

Each of these variations in corrective measures can be combined at any time to ensure that your dog is sufficiently observant and responsive to meet your requirements.

(2) The dog who lags may well require a little more thought before considering the action to be taken. Dogs will lag behind for various reasons.

A tall man with a very small dog will have a problem if he tries to walk at a smart pace. Every step from such an owner may equal half a dozen steps from his little dog and there is no way that the animal can keep up with his human companion. The owner must, therefore, control his speed to suit the size of his dog. The overweight, unfit or ageing dog must also be given due consideration and again the speed should be set to suit the individual case. A little extra speed and a diet would, of course, rectify any overweight situation.

Many dogs lag because of a lack of confidence. Some may have received an unsympathetic introduction to the collar and lead and others may be of a nervous disposition. They may be quite unhappy among the activities of the outside world. Children running down the street, or noisy, smelly lorries trundling past may well be the cause of a dog's uncertainty. Such a cause requires understanding, a bit of coaxing and a great deal of encouragement. A gentle but sharp tug on the lead along with an encouraging tone of voice will do a lot to dispel the dog's anxiety. Get him to understand by your actions and tone of voice that it is fun to be by your side. Stop every now and again to tell him how great he is, but do not stop whilst he is lagging. Give him that gentle tug with encouragement then when he is walking with you stop to chat him up.

Your dog may well need encouragement and understanding but he will also require a measure of firmness until he gains sufficient confidence to stride out beside you without a care in the world.

(3) The dog who stops and sniffs at every opportunity can be cured if you are able to anticipate these actions and nip them in the bud.

By observing his habits you should know when to expect your dog to stop and sniff at a gate-post, lamp-post or such like and thus be prepared to stop him doing so.

In the initial stages of corrective training you should catch him as he is pausing to sniff; give him a sharp tug on the lead as you speed up to get him past the distraction. Immediate praise is then necessary to let him know you are pleased with him for reacting to your sharp tug.

After a few such corrective tugs on the lead you can start to encourage your dog past these distractions by using your voice — 'Come on son, come on,' should be quite sufficient. Get his attention on to yourself and away from the interesting smell.

It will, of course, be realised that dogs require time to attend to their toilet requirements and many dogs are expected to carry out this function whilst on the lead. There is a time and a place for everything and your dog will soon understand that you have stopped walking to give him the opportunity to do the needful.

Whilst your dog is on the lead you are in an ideal position to control the situation and if you have problems they will not go away without effort on your part. Your contribution must be based on understanding, encouragement and firmness in appropriate measures to suit the character of your canine companion.

Approach to lead handling

Your approach to lead handling can be a major factor in your success or failure at loose lead walking.

During the various stages of training both hands come into play with the right hand holding the end of the lead and also, when necessary, taking up the excess. The left hand is the one which controls the situation.

Your right thumb should be in the loop at the end of the lead with the remainder of the loop in your clenched hand, any excess lead being folded back and held with the loop. The full length of lead can thus be attained at any time by releasing the hold without losing control of the looped end.

In this way, the left hand is free to apply control as and when it is required. The lead may be allowed to slip through the left hand at will, to be held firm only when that sharp tug is required, then immediately released.

When your dog is fully trained to walk nicely at your left side you may find it more convenient to hold the lead in your left hand. It may also be

The first stage in holding a lead during training.

advisable to minimise the amount of slack lead between yourself and your dog. If there is just sufficient lead in use to create a minimum of slackness for comfort, your dog will realise that any excess movement out of line will cause a tightening of the slip collar. This can help to give your dog a greater feeling of responsibility.

Holding the lead correctly in the right hand with the left hand ready for action as required.

One convenient and effective method of holding the lead in the left hand is to slip three fingers into the loop at the end of the lead, leaving your thumb and index finger free to control your use of the lead. Let the rest of the lead drop then assess the length you wish to work with. Loop the lead over your hand so that you are holding it between your thumb and index finger. This is the point of control with the desired length of lead between your hand and the dog's collar.

To start and finish with a sit

To start your loose lead walking with your dog in the sit position, then to have him sit when you stop is, for general purposes, an unnecessary refinement which is generally instilled at training clubs. It can be a valuable addition to your repertoire and is included for those who are interested in training for competitive work or feel that this additional measure of control is advisable.

The method of teaching your dog to sit is fully described in Chapter 8 and this procedure should be fully applied before adding sits to your loose lead routine.

Assuming your dog knows the meaning of the instruction to sit he can, therefore, be directed to sit at your left side. Your own attitude is now dependent on your dog's mental disposition. If he becomes inhibited at the sit he may well require a great deal of encouragement to move off with you as you instruct him to *'Heel.'* If he is of an excitable nature he will require a more sobering approach to the instruction 'Heel.'

Whatever his nature make sure you have his attention. Remember that his name is the attention getter when applied with the correct tone of voice, especially when it is given in the form of a question, *'Ben? Heel.'*

When you stop in your walking you should, as you are about to halt, again get your dog's attention with '*Ben?*' followed by the instruction '*Sit*' as you come to a stop. The use of his name interrogatively will ensure that his attention is fully with you and he will soon learn to anticipate the sit instruction.

Single-handed lead control is quite adequate for a trained dog.

Kapra walks nicely off the lead with the appropriate encouragement.

Misha, the reluctant walker, seems to have perfected the art of lagging behind.

8 Teaching Your Dog to Stay

There are many reasons why a dog should be taught to stay, either in the sit, stand or down position. A veterinary examination will normally require your dog to be under control in any of these positions; the same can be said of your own need to examine your dog from time to time.

To have your dog sit while you are waiting to cross the road or while you are having a chat with somebody can give you the opportunity to concentrate on the situation at hand without the inconvenience of an unruly dog. Very wet or muddy conditions may seem unsuitable for having a dog sit or go down when you require a measure of control, so to

Brandy sits patiently at the kerb as he waits to cross the road.

With their dogs at the down these owners can have a leisurely chat.

have him standing can be a useful alternative. To leave your dog in the down position or to have the ability of downing him from a distance is probably the most useful of the three stay positions. A dog is generally more at ease in the down position and can be left with much greater certainty than in either of the other positions.

The sit and down requirements are very much akin to the stand position but require a different approach. We will give the training requirements for the sit and down positions first consideration.

The objective is twofold.

(a) The dog's instant response to the owner's instruction to sit or go down.
(b) The requirement to stay in that position until released by the owner.

Although formal training methods are normally required to obtain an instant response an observant owner can make use of a more natural approach to training. This has already been discussed on page 28.

When considering objective (b) the question arises: How long should a dog be expected to remain in the stay position? The build-up of time and distance must be taken very slowly with a corresponding growth of confidence — your own confidence that your dog will remain in the selected position until you return; the dog's confidence that you will return every time and be in a suitable frame of mind to let him know how pleased you are. Remember that your confidence can only be built on his confidence. An overconfident owner can ruin a good dog.

To give some idea of the length of time you can expect a dog to stay in the one position it might be helpful to give details of the competitive requirements for the highest standards of Obedience Tests or Working Trials.

(a) Stand Stay — One minute duration with the owners about ten paces from and with their backs to their dogs.

(b) Sit Stay — Two minutes duration with the owners out of the dogs' sight.

(c) Down Stay — Ten minutes duration with the owners out of the dogs' sight.

These details should help you to assess the limit of duration for each of the stay positions in training.

A class of pet dogs sits in line after a course of training.

Training to sit

As well as using natural situations when they occur, semi-natural situations can also be created. Whilst your dog is in front of you, or you can move to stand in front of him, get his attention on your face or high up on your body. In achieving this it will become natural for your dog to sit; he can see you so much easier this way.

In the initial stages, do not ask your dog to sit until he is going voluntarily into that position, then tell him in a gentle manner to sit. Food can

A very attentive sit with Freida's alertness directed on her owner's eyes.

be an excellent inducement if it is used to draw his head up so that it is much easier for him to go automatically into the sit position. You again say 'Sit' as he is going into that position, then give him his titbit as soon as his bottom hits the deck. Dogs who have been allowed in the past to jump up at their owners will probably use occasions like this to continue the practice. Although expert handlers can prevent this habit whilst using the semi-natural approach to sitting, it may be better for the novice to avoid the technique if such problems interfere.

The stricter training routine can now be considered and this approach should be carried out with your dog on the lead whilst he is standing or walking by your left side. During the early stages it is not necessary to bring him close to your side, you can step in beside him to achieve the desired position. With your lead held short in your right hand and your left hand nestled in at the top and left side of your dog's croup push his rear end down and towards you, at the same time pulling steadily on the lead to draw his head up. Whilst you are starting to apply this pressure at the rear end together with tension at the front, speak gently to your dog. 'That's a good boy,' should be sufficient, but as soon as he starts moving into the sit position give a soft but firm instruction to 'Sit, Ben,' with greater emphasis on the 'Sit.' Immediately he is in the sit position give him praise. This should be gentle praise with fondling of his head or neck, but make sure that he does not attempt to stand up or lie down. Again during the early stages a five-second compulsory sit will probably be long enough before letting him free and giving unbounded praise.

In time (this varies according to your abilities and your dog's reactions) you will find that by touching your dog on the left side of his croup he will immediately go into the sit position. When he has reached this stage, you

Physically assisting Digger into the sit position.

Completing the assisted sit, pulling up and back on the lead and pushing down at the croup.

can give the sit instruction as you bend over to touch his croup; at this point verbal instruction will start to replace your physical movements.

It is preferable not to progress too far until your dog is prepared to respond immediately to the verbal instruction to sit, and it is probably advisable to continue to maintain control on the lead. Any reluctance to respond should be countered immediately with a second instruction to coincide with the physical assistance already described. This, of course, must not be carried out in anger, but with firmness and then praise on completion of the movement.

The sit-stay

For domestic purposes it is not important to have a dog sit and stay for a period whilst you walk away and leave him. The purpose of sit and stay training is to achieve a steady dog so that he will sit for a reasonable period whilst you attend to your immediate business. It is also another control feature which helps to give your dog a sense of responsibility.

Dogs can react to stay training in many different ways. Some are excitable and always want to be doing something, others are rather

Ensuring that Digger settles contentedly in the sit position.

nervous or possessive of their owners and have a fear of being left. Then there are the dogs who could not care less and will forget what they are supposed to be doing, seeming to lack a sense of responsibility.

The owner's own approach will also have considerable effect. To be too forceful with your voice or physical actions can cause uncertainty in the dog. To be too soft in your approach will give your dog the impression that you do not mean it. Care must be taken to use the correct measure of authority to suit your particular dog's temperament.

To achieve a comfortable and settled situation in the early stages, which will ensure that your dog remains sitting when required, you should stand straddled over your dog without touching his body with your legs. This action should be carried out as soon as your dog is in the sitting position. Stand straddled facing the same direction as your dog, or if he is a very small fellow you can kneel. This allows you to fondle his neck with both hands at will and yet you can take your hands away and he will remain in that position. With the gentle but firm instruction 'Sit and stay, Ben,' followed by a gentler 'That's a good boy,' you will let him know that you are pleased with his performance.

The use of the gentler 'That's a good boy' may well encourage your

Digger is nicely settled but the owner is ready in case he thinks of moving.

dog to respond by trying to get up for more praise. This is the first test of your control and he must be stopped from doing so. You need to anticipate this possible move and be ready to counter it immediately with physical assistance to stay sitting along with the instruction given firmly to 'Sit and stay, Ben.' This again is followed by the gentle praise 'That's a good boy.' It is only when he remains steady after the praise has been given that you can consider moving back half a step from your dog.

You may well ask why one should give praise if it is likely to cause the dog to get up — a sound question. Without the application of repeated praise many owners are found to become stern and uncompromising in their attitude. This may not appear to have any effect on their dogs in the earlier stages of training but often creates breaks from the stay position as training progresses. The giving of gentle praise creates the opportunity to correct the dog at the first sign of any undesired movement whilst the owner is in a position to prevent absolute failure. Thereby, the dog is stress free and a good foundation is being created for stability as training progresses.

When you feel that your dog is settled and you are confident that he will remain sitting you can start to walk round him. Whilst moving

A hand signal keeps Kim in place.

round him continue to instruct 'Sit and stay, Ben,' followed by that little bit of praise. (It is important not to use the dog's name at the beginning of the instruction or he will expect a recall. This mistake is often made by novice handlers.) Visual signals are also of great value. A show of the flat of your hand along with the 'Sit and stay, Ben' instruction can act as a stabilising influence. However, if you use visual signals make sure your dog can see them. Too often, I see owners at training sessions giving signals above or behind their dogs' heads where it is impossible for the dogs to see and interpret such signals.

For domestic purposes there is little reason to leave your dog sitting whilst you go away any distance or out of sight. To leave him at the down stay is certainly of much more value. If any owner wishes to train for the 'sit out of sight' then I suggest that the down stay training principles be applied to the sit and stay.

Each time you instruct your dog to stay you are applying a positive and definite attitude to ensure that your dog understands precisely what is expected of him. Any indecision on your part will create a confused canine mind — he will be unsure and this will lead to mistakes. He will break when he should be staying and will, no doubt, be expected to take the blame.

Until your dog is very sound on the stay-sit you should return to him at the end of every stay exercise — *do not* call him to you as this is likely to cause anticipation and he may well break of his own accord in the future.

When you are ready to break the stay pick up the end of the lead, or if you are at a stage when the lead can be removed during the stay, use an excited tone of voice along with any appropriate physical movements to let him know that he is being freed from the sit position.

To give a dog freedom from any controlled situation I usually start the sentence with 'OK son . . .' It is the excited tone of voice together with your physical movements which gives him the cue to break. The words are relatively unimportant.

Training to go down

There are many opportunities to use the natural method of teaching the meaning of the instruction to go down. Every time your dog lies down to rest, the words 'Down, Ben, that's a good boy,' can be used in the same manner as with the sit training.

The semi-natural method can also be employed, with food or a favourite toy as an inducement. Get down on the floor beside your dog (this is generally an indoor training method) and when you are down at his level you can encourage him to try and reach the inducement, whatever it be. With the tempting article in your hand, at floor level, your dog may lie down to try to get it from you. The moment he is down let him

Tara going down on
verbal and visual
instruction.

have the inducement along with the usual praise 'That's a good boy.' In
this way your dog will soon learn to go down to your hand to get his
reward and it is at this stage that you give the instruction 'Down, Ben,'
followed by praise.

You can use the natural and the semi-natural methods but still use the
stricter training routines to achieve your objective. With the latter it may
not be necessary to hold your dog on the lead, but rather than have a
situation which you cannot control it may be an advisable precaution to
leave the lead attached to his collar.

The initial training should be carried out from the sit position. It is
much easier to teach a dog to go down from the sit than from the stand
position. As the down is a very submissive position for a dog he might
object strongly to being forcibly put down from the stand position.

Have your dog sitting at your left side and get down to his level (you
may find it easier to kneel). Put your left arm over his shoulder so that
your left hand is placed behind his left pastern. At the same time put your
right hand behind his right pastern. Push his front feet forward from
underneath him, or lift his front feet forward so that he will drop onto his
chest. At the same time let your own body drop to rest on your left elbow.
As you are doing this use a very soothing voice to tell him he is a good
dog.

Whilst your dog is in the down position be positive in telling him to
'Stay.' If he is restless and would prefer to get up, maintain your position
over him for a very short period; five seconds is probably long enough.

Preparing to put Isla
into the down position.

Isla on the way down.

Isla settling in the down
position.

When you let him up be equally positive in telling him he can get up as
you release him.

By using firmness and gentle praise your dog will soon anticipate your
actions when you put your left arm over his shoulder to put him down. At
this stage use the verbal instruction 'Down' as he is going into that position without any physical assistance from yourself.

Concentrate on achieving an instant response to the instruction
'Down' from the sit position when you are standing beside or in front of
your dog. Only when you have achieved a guaranteed and quick response
should you think of putting your dog down from the stand or a walking
situation. He may well respond to the change-over immediately, but if
not then make the change-over more gradual by instructing 'Sit' then
immediately his bottom touches the ground indicate your requirement of
the down position.

Hand and body signals can again be a convenient aid to an attentive
response, but make sure that your signals are going to be an inducement
to go down.

The down-stay

This is the most comfortable position in which to leave a dog, but he must be completely at ease and you should make no attempt to move away from him if you sense any uncertainty on his part. It helps, and it is a good guide, if you can leave your dog looking comfortable and resting with his rear end on its side.

Duke, the GSD, is down at ease and unlikely to move but Zula, the Ridgeback, has other interests and could be in an unsettled frame of mind.

Any uneasiness should be countered with a soothing tone of voice combined with alertness on your part to any attempt he may make to get up. You will, therefore, require to be close enough, and in a suitable position, to apply the firm instruction '*Stay*' as you exert a little pressure on his shoulder with your hand. Do not forget the gentle praise, 'That's a good boy.' If you have allowed your dog to get up you are either too late in taking preventive action or not sufficiently attentive.

Whilst your dog is in the down position the firmness of your voice along with gentle reassurance is most important. '*Stay, Ben*, that's a good boy' is all that is required, but the tone of the verbal expressions and the manner of the visual signals can help to make or break a good stable dog.

Finishing the down-stay is carried out in a similar maner to that of the sit-stay, with a positive and appreciative recognition of your dog's co-operation.

Distance and time require a long slow build-up with care being taken to ensure that you are in a position to counter any distraction. If you leave your dog at the down whilst training in the park and you see another dog coming into sight do not wait to see what happens. Go back to your dog and prevent a problem from arising; remember that your dog is in a submissive position and he will feel very vulnerable.

When you can walk away safely for a distance of twenty paces or so you can try moving out of sight, behind a tree, round the side of a building or even lie down in long grass. The important point is that although you may be out of your dog's sight you should be in a position to watch him until you have well-founded confidence that he will not move.

The principles throughout the down-stay are similar to that of the sit-stay, but a well-settled dog at the down-stay who has the confidence that his owner will always come back to him has possibly one of the most valuable canine assets.

To take greater advantage of your down-stay training you should be able to stop and down your dog anywhere. He may be five yards from you or he may be fifty yards away. Something may take his attention and the attraction could well be beyond your measure of control to get him to come directly back to you. For instance, he may see another dog and want to give chase. The conflict of interests may be too great to achieve a recall but to keep him from running towards the other dog can serve the purpose, sending him into the down position or getting him to stand where he is.

Training your dog to go down at any reasonable distance can best be carried out when you are out for a walk with him, whilst he is being given freedom off the lead. (He must, of course, have been trained to respond to the instruction to go down whilst by your side before venturing into a situation where there is distance between you and himself.) When you are walking and your dog is about five to ten paces from you, call his name to get his immediate attention. As soon as he heeds you, start walking towards him; this will prevent him from coming to you. As you start walking towards him instruct him to go down; do not be irritated if he does not respond immediately — the situation is new to him — but he must go down when you reach him.

As your dog learns this new routine of complete freedom being interrupted by the instruction to go down his response will improve. Avoid strong clashes of interest if possible until you have attained a high standard of proficiency with immediate response being guaranteed from varying distances.

The stand-stay

Training your dog to stand is a relatively simple process although it brings in the principles already discussed in the sit and down training. The training is simplified by the fact that, for domestic purposes, there is no need to walk away and leave him staying in the stand position.

Again training should be carried out with the dog on the lead, starting from a standing, sitting or down position.

If your dog is already standing hold your lead in your right hand with the collar attachment under his muzzle. Place your left hand under and slightly lifting his muzzle as you stand in front and facing your dog. Move backwards as you draw him forward for a step or two. As he is moving instruct him firmly but gently, '*Stand*,' and as soon as you stop his forward movement instruct him, '*Stay*,' then give him a little praise.

If this praise induces thoughts of further movement to sit or lie down repeat your backward movement to retain a steady standing position. If he wants to continue moving forward restrain him with your hand under his muzzle whilst you give a little gentle praise.

When you feel that your dog is steady and you can walk round him start to feel over his body with the flat of your hands, also feel over his shoulders, across the flanks of his body, his croup and down his hindquarters. Get your dog used to being handled and to retain a controlled stand-stay position.

The process of training the stand from a sitting or down position is the same in detail as given from the standing position, but in the early stages it is likely that your dog will try to revert to his starting position. It is just a case of drawing him forward a step or two every time he thinks of sitting or lying down. Again do not wait until he has made his move, catch him at the thinking stage or as he starts to move. He will soon understand your requirements.

Finishing the stand-stay exercise is carried out in the same manner as that of the other stay positions. Let your dog know in a positive and appreciative manner that you are pleased with him.

9 A Training Programme

The applications for control training which are described in Chapters 6, 7 and 8 are the foundation for a happy and sociable canine companionship, and the various elements within each of these applications for control have a particular sequence with certain elements being common to various control disciplines.

One of the principal reasons for a dog owner's failure to achieve his training objectives is lack of appreciation that the dog's advancement should be regulated to suit his progress and that each stage or step in the training routine should be consolidated before pressing on with the next. That exceptional circumstances may demand a reappraisal of progress and the need to go back a step or two, or even further, to correct an undesirable situation must be appreciated.

To achieve progress any training programme requires objectives where advancement is controlled by a series of intermediate targets. To ensure that these targets are linked in a satisfactory manner a training sequence has been devised to help you determine your own rate of progress.

It is important that throughout you do not try to progress beyond your dog's present stage of competence but to work for and consolidate at each target stage.

The programme which follows is based on an eight-week course of training which is at present being used within a class situation where twelve dogs and their owners receive a one hour per week period of tuition. The owners are expected to practise at home and consolidate in preparation for the next session.

It is suggested that you follow the instructions given in the foregoing sections and then apply the training programme over an eight-week period to achieve a sound foundation of control over your canine companion. Before you begin, though, your dog or puppy should already be accustomed to his collar and lead.

If at any time you are unable to achieve a target within any of the control disciplines in a satisfactory manner it is essential that you return at least to the previous stage of training. Real progress can only be attained via a sound and guaranteed performance at each stage.

Remember that repeated success is required to guarantee its continuation.

THE PROGRAMME

1. TRAINING EXERCISE — *To come back when called*

The objective — To ensure that your dog will give you his full attention when required and will respond to the call to come back to you.

The targets

1a Your dog should respond to a little tug on the lead and willingly move with you as you call him whilst you are moving backwards for a few seconds.

1b Whilst on the long line your dog should also respond as in (1a) but from a greater distance.

1c Whilst on the lead or long line he should give you his full attention immediately you call his name — without the need to tug at the end of the lead or line.

1d With your dog on the lead you should be able to keep his attention sufficiently to ensure that he will keep his eyes on you as long as you move round for a spell of about ten seconds.

1e When on a long line, left free and at a line length away from your dog, he should respond immediately to the call and come back to you.

1f Returning to target (1d) your dog should be prepared to sit in front of you when he comes in from the call to 'Come'.

1g Returning to target (1e) your dog should sit in front of you from a distance recall.

1h Whilst he is completely free your dog should return to you immediately he is called and should also sit in front.

2. TRAINING EXERCISE — *Loose lead walking*

The objective — To have your dog walk reasonably close and level with your left leg. He should be attentive, walk at your speed and maintain the close position as you change directions. He should also be prepared to move off from the sitting position and also sit immediately you halt.

NOTE — All movements to be carried out with your dog on the lead.

The targets

2a You should be able to hold and handle your lead in the correct manner.

2b You should be able to keep your dog's attention sufficiently to ensure that he will keep his eyes on you as you walk round for about ten seconds. He should also respond immediately to a sharp corrective tug when required. Encouragement and titbits as inducements to be used to the full. A tight lead should be avoided at all times.

2c You should be able to walk forward with your dog reasonably close to your left side with encouragement and titbits as required for a spell of about fifteen seconds. Walk in a straight line or large left hand circle.

2d Your dog should now be prepared to sit when instructed on completion of loose lead walking.

2e Your dog should be prepeared to sit before commencement of loose lead walking.

2f Periods of loose lead walking should be possible where encouragement is limited or titbits withheld.

2g Changes in direction with left, right and about-turns should be attainable with the build up of attention from the previous sequence of targets.

3 and 4 TRAINING EXERCISES — *Sit or down stay*

The objectives — To ensure that your dog will go into the desired position and remain in that position for a specified period of time. Your dog should remain in that position until you return and finish the exercise.

The targets

3a Your dog should stay *sitting* for a few seconds when you put him in that position and whilst you stand straddled over him and facing in the same direction.

4a Your dog should stay in the *down* position for a few seconds when you put him in that position and whilst you kneel at his right side or stand beside him.

3b He should then stay sitting/down for about ten seconds whilst

4b you are standing in front of him, also whilst you walk round him at the end of the lead. At no time should he move from the sit/down position until permitted.

3c Your dog should be prepared to sit/down immediately you give

4c the appropriate instruction whilst he is at your left side without giving him physical assistance.

3d He should stay sitting/down for half a minute whilst you are

4d at the end of a loose lead.

3e Your dog should always remain sitting/down whilst you return
4e and stand by his right side.
3f He should remain sitting/down whilst you walk away for about
4f ten paces, face him for ten seconds or so then return to him.
3g He should be prepared to sit/down for graduated periods of up
4g to two minutes' duration whilst you stand away at distances up to
   twenty paces.

COURSE WEEK	One	Two	Three	Four	Five	Six	Seven	Eight
Recall (1) Lead	a	b	c	d	e	f	g	h
Walking (2)	a	a	b	c	d	e	f	g
Sit-Stay (3) Down	a	a	b	c	d	e	f	g
Stay (4) Stand for	—	a	b	c	d	e	f	g
Examination	—	—	—	x	x	x	x	x

Part III — The Situations

10 Walking Your Dog

Without the achievement of the control described in the previous chapters, many problems can occur when a dog is taken out for a walk or is allowed to be loose for a period of free exercise.

These problems can be avoided by anticipation, or by correctly sizing up the situation, or by choosing the right approach to neutralise any clash of interests between yourself and your dog.   A pleasant walk in a suburban area with your dog walking free and nicely by your side can easily turn into a disaster if a cat emerges from a garden gate and darts across the road. Or a stray dog may decide to give your dog some attention with similar results. Situations like this, especially when you are not anticipating such events, can cause your normally well-behaved dog to give chase or run into the middle of the road just to protect itself. There is nothing clever about taking your dog out for a walk without his lead and to do so in a suburban area can make the prospect of human and canine tragedy very real.

When I am out for a walk I take time to observe the actions and reactions of all dogs. Being the owner of two German Shepherds (Alsatians)

A suburban walk with Brandy is a pleasure.

the reactions of some dogs can be rather disconcerting to their owners who up to now have felt confident enough to give their dogs complete freedom. My own dogs can be on their leads, perfectly well behaved, but the sight of the very dominant male German Shepherd is often sufficient for another dog, which is on the loose, to cross the road or to turn back and refuse to pass my dogs. On most occasions the owners are quite ineffective in trying to call their dogs back to them, yet other dogs who are on the lead are quite happy to pass and very rarely show any signs of apprehension.

Caro and Isla enjoying the freedom of the beach.

When my dogs are off the lead in areas where freedom can be enjoyed to the full, I remain constantly observant. In wooded areas where vision is restricted, the first indication of an approaching dog is often from the reaction of my own dogs. Isla, my bitch, would probably note the existence of another dog in the vicinity and would not be bothered by its presence but she would soon see off an amorous male. Caro, being a dominant male, and especially with Isla present, will stand four square facing the appropriate direction as soon as he senses another dog.

To ask Caro to come back to me in such a situation would be unfair; he would come back if I demanded it but would feel that he was turning his back on an adversary leaving his vulnerable rear end open to attack. To ask Caro to go down would be creating a submissive situation; this would be completely against his nature and again would be unfair. A third alternative, more in keeping with his character, would be to tell him to stay.

Although Caro's training is such that he would comply with any of these alternatives the command to stay would be most appropriate to a dog of his character. I could then walk up to him and maintain the degree of authority required for the situation, possibly putting him on the lead if the actions of the other dog warrant this measure of control. Under similar circumstances I could recall Isla in to me and find that she would be more than happy to comply with my request.

Some dogs under these conditions would immediately run towards the other dog. In such a situation the average dog owner does not normally have sufficient control to call his dog back. However, with suitable training the dog can be successfully instructed to stop and go down until the owner reaches him when he can exert relaxed control over the situation. It must be recognised that a dog in full flight is extremely difficult to stop and the earlier the command is given the greater chance there is of success.

Owners meet and their controlled dogs cause no problems.

Many owners of placid easy-going dogs fail to recognise the potential danger of allowing their pets to fraternise with strange dogs. To meet a friend or acquaintance with his dog and to know that a friendly relationship exists between the dogs is one thing, but to allow your dog to befriend a completely strange dog can be asking for trouble. In fact to allow your dog to mix and play with any other dog when your control or that of the other dog's owner is suspect, is going to create a situation which is likely to be regretted with both dogs getting the blame for apparent disobedience.

Another two owners meet and this could spell trouble.

The loose or stray dog who pesters another dog when out with his owner is a problem which few people seem able to handle without causing aggressiveness in their own dogs. It is quite a natural reaction for an owner, with his own dog on the lead, to shout and threaten or to try and hit the other dog with a stick or a stone, but it is one which brings out canine defensive instincts and can cause his dog to show aggression to all other dogs — and at any time. In a sense the dog is being taught to defend his owner and will respond by showing this aggression at the most inappropriate times.

To overcome this problem, I find it best to have my dog on the lead and turn in such a manner that he will follow me round so that I can give the other dog a back heel kick, under the chin if properly aimed. I try to do this without giving any indication to my own dog of my intentions — and am usually successful.

Some dogs have a very strong natural instinct to chase, be it another dog, a cat, a rabbit or some form of game or farm animal. The inclination to chase can also include bicycles, motor cars or people. In fact some dogs will chase anything which moves at speed, it somehow seems to be a challenge. It must be remembered that previous experiences are going to affect your dog. If he has been allowed to chase in the past, the instinct will be strengthened by the pleasure it has given him and the lack of successful preventive measures on the part of the owner.

To chase a cat can take a dog into other people's gardens or across a road, thereby becoming a nuisance or a danger to everybody. To chase a bicycle or a motor car can be considered as a most dangerous pastime and cannot be tolerated. To allow a dog the opportunity to chase sheep or cattle can only be considered as a gross inconsideration for both animals and farmer, quite apart from the legal aspect of such an activity and also the possibility of your dog being shot. To chase certain species of game may be natural and quite in order, but for the domestic pet this is generally another indication of the owner's lack of control or responsibility. All in all, to own a chaser is a responsibility which cannot be taken too lightly and this requires anticipation, constant observation and a very strong measure of control on the part of the owner.

To completely suppress the chasing instinct in a dog would be rather inconsiderate but it can well be channelled into an enjoyable and purposeful activity. To throw a ball, a stick or some other suitable article can provide a very enjoyable outlet for excess energy for any dog, be it a chaser or not, giving both mental and physical exercise, especially when the thrown article lands in undergrowth where it requires the dog's scenting ability to find it.

Although this form of activity will not, in itself, stop a dog from chasing at the wrong time it does help to act as a safety valve. It is advisable to always bear in mind that a dog can only chase when he is given the opportunity and it is therefore the owner's responsibility to ensure that these opportunities are given at his bidding and not at his dog's.

The instinct of the chase being fully satisfied.

11 Travelling with Your Dog

Car travel can be considered these days as an essential part of a dog's life if he is to be treated as a member of the family. He is a companion and, to obtain the full measure of that companionship, your dog will be eager to accompany you whenever he gets the opportunity.

Some dogs really enjoy being in a car. I know only too well the looks of disappointment and sometimes of disbelief on the occasions that I go out in the car and my dogs are left at home. I can go to work with a briefcase in my hand and they do not bother, but to go out to the car in casual wear or even dressed in the evening there is bitter disappointment if they are not allowed to accompany me.

When we travel a distance to compete in working trials the car becomes a dog kennel and the dogs often sleep overnight on their own in the vehicle (there is a fringe benefit here — they make an efficient deterrent to any would-be car thief).

A well-behaved travelling canine companion can certainly be a pleasure and an asset but the dog who makes a nuisance of himself in the car is a danger to the driver, the passengers and other road users. No driver can give his full attention to the road ahead if he is distracted by the antics of his canine companion.

What then are the problems posed by dogs in motor cars? Let us start with the distressing problem of car sickness which, unfortunately, discourages many a dog owner and results in a number of pets being left at home when they could be out enjoying the companionship they deserve.

Car sickness

Although many puppies never experience car sickness, the owners of those who are less fortunate often find the situation rather difficult to cope with.

Some owners hope that by leaving the puppy at home maturity in itself will eliminate the problem; unfortunately this is seldom the case.

The first day with your puppy will probably involve a car journey home from the breeding kennel, and most likely this will be his first experience of car travel. The stress and uncertainty of leaving the only home he has ever known — along with yourself as a complete stranger replacing his own family, and the effects of the car's movements may well result in a bout of car sickness or an excess of saliva. This first journey may well be the most important of his life and the more you can minimise the stress the better. A sedative prescribed by your vet and administered at the appropriate time should make the little fellow rather drowsy. Towels on your knee or on the seat where he is resting would be a wise precaution and help to put your own mind at rest.

However, if you find that your puppy is going to be troubled with car sickness, be it bouts of sickness or constant dribbling which leaves the whole chest and front paws of your puppy in a wet matted mess, then action must be taken to get him over this troublesome period as quickly as possible.

Ideally, he should be given the opportunity to experience a car journey every day, even if it is only a short trip round the block. If you can hold him on your knee whilst somebody else drives so much the better. Your puppy's nervous system is upset and the cushioning of any movement will help him, along with the fact that you can comfort him during troublesome periods. Again, whether you hold your puppy or settle him in the back of the car you will require to use old towels or newspapers, or both, to protect both the inside of the car and yourself.

To take the puppy for a ride after a meal would be courting disaster; the best time to make those short excursions would be just *before* feeding time when the previous meal has been well digested. It would be beneficial if you refrained from feeding him immediately after the journey; give him quarter of an hour or so to relax before presenting him with his dish of food.

When you take your puppy out in the car you may find that he will begin to dribble before you even reach the end of your road. If this is the case try settling him in the car for a short period whilst it is stationary. You can sit with him or leave him if he can be trusted not to get up to mischief — a few such spells in the car without movement should help to give him confidence.

As a car driver you can do much to help your puppy get over his sickness problems; cornering at too great a speed, fast acceleration and sharp braking all contribute to the stress he feels in the car. A bumpy or undulating road taken at an unsuitable speed can also unsettle a youngster and ruin a lot of good groundwork.

Remember that a car-sick puppy may take some time to cure. It is your care and consideration which can shorten the period of inconvenience to yourself and your puppy.

The more adult problems

The problems which are created by dogs in motor cars can be put into three significant categories.

(1) The antics of a dog whilst the car is being driven along the road.

(2) The dog's attitude and activities whilst the car is parked and un-attended.

(3) Scrambling out of the car when it stops.

The first and most important consideration is the dog's attitude in the car whilst it is being driven on the road. A badly behaved dog is certainly a danger to all and that point must be foremost in our minds when we consider the measure of control which is required.

It is essential that your dog understands and is prepared to respond to your requirements; at no time should your attention be diverted from the job in hand, i.e. driving your car. If a problem does arise you should drive into a quiet side street, park, make your intentions positively understood, and ensure that the dog is fully responsive before returning to your original route.

Where your dog sits or lies in the car may not seem to be important. He probably likes to view the passing scenery or traffic and whilst this keeps his interest, it will prevent him from taking the driver's attention. He may prefer to lie and sleep during the journey and this, too, is to the driver's benefit.

In a saloon car the viewing type of dog is more suited to the rear seat; dogs who like to lie and sleep are also suited to rear seat accommodation but they could also be settled on the floor area of the front passenger seat. However, a dog settled on the floor must be one who can be trusted to stay in that position or else be under the control of the front seat passenger. It should be noted that rear-engined cars, which do not have the separating gear box cover between the driver and passenger, are not really suited to a dog being settled by the front seat. It would be only too easy for the dog to obstruct the operating pedals and thereby cause a disaster.

To have a dog settled on the front seat or on the lap of the front seat passenger can prove to be a dangerous situation if drastic evasive action has to be taken by the driver to prevent an accident.

It will, of course, be obvious that very large breeds cannot be accommodated in the front of the car.

Estate cars are ideally suited to dog transport and the installation of a dog guard will ensure that any canine activity is restricted to the designated area.

It should now be realised that an unruly dog in a car is quite unacceptable and that training to prevent such a situation is necessary. It should also be understood that a dog who has not received basic training in desirable canine behaviour outside the car is unlikely to respond to instructions from his owner whilst travelling in the vehicle.

It is, therefore, essential that to go down on command is an automatic reaction required from any dog who is going to be under the sole control of the driver. However, to have a dog respond on command in varying situations whilst out of the car is no guarantee that such instructions will be respected whilst the car is being driven. The training may well have to be practised inside the stationary car before venturing out on the open road without a controlling passenger.

The second problem is that of the attitude and activities of your dog in a parked and unattended car. This problem can also be divided into two parts with the first concerning the destructive dog.

Unfortunately, destructiveness is usually related to boredom and it is advisable, from the travelling aspect as well as that of parking, to give the active dog a fair amount of exercise to take some of the exuberance out of his system. However, wilful destruction in a parked car is similar to destruction at home; the reasoning and the treatment are the same. You have to catch your dog thinking about it, or in the act, to achieve any measure of success; to punish him after the event is generally quite useless. To leave your dog with some of his toys may be of value but a piece of car wiring or a strap dangling may take his attention and a little tug with his teeth may start a chain of events which can end up with expensive repairs or a marked devaluation of your car.

One answer to the problem could be to put your dog into the car whilst he is in a boisterous mood and will be easily bored with the lack of activity. You should then sit in the driving seat and adjust the mirror so that you can watch your dog without him realising that you are fully aware of his activities. Just sit and watch for the slightest indication of destructive behaviour, then voice a strong rebuke immediately. Do not turn round unless it is absolutely necessary — let him wonder how you knew that he was up to mischief.

You could, of course, move away from your car and then return to it from another direction so that your dog would not be aware of your presence. The direction of the wind is important and you should walk away into the wind then return on the leeward side so that your scent does not betray your presence; again you are in a position to act as soon as there is any sign of destructive activities. Pet pens can be the answer to a number of travelling problems (see page 127).

The other problem is that of protection. Some dogs are overly protective when left in the car and it is most difficult to moderate this activity without killing off the instinct. You should remember that a dog who protects his owner's car is a great asset and it may be a situation which should be allowed to run its course, although there should not be any need to encourage this attitude whilst you are present. You should demand a more respectful attitude to passers-by whilst you are in or beside the car; that is, your dog should understand that he does not require to protect the car when you are present.

I find with my own dogs that it helps for a peaceful existence if I cover some of the windows on the basis of 'what they do not see they will not bark at'. Although this certainly works with some dogs it is not a guaranteed cure.

Dogs without patience or training can be a danger to a passing motorist.

Dogs in training and waiting patiently for permission to move.

We come now to the third problem. Travelling becomes such a pleasure to most dogs that there is rarely any difficulty in getting a dog to go into a car, especially when it is realised that the alternative is to be left at home. However, many dogs ignore the niceties of alighting from a car at the end of a journey. They make a mad scramble to be first out of the car when it stops and a door is opened.

This is a situation which should not be tolerated. Apart from the dangers from and to other traffic, it is just another example of an owner's failure to control the situation.

An extension of the stay training is all that is required to achieve a more orderly exit from the car, with your dog awaiting permission to leave and on the lead if the circumstances warrant such a precaution. It must be remembered, however, that a dog is unlikely to stay when he is keyed up to get out of the car if he has not been given the basic training in that exercise.

12 Your Dog in the Garden

It has often been said that dogs and gardeners are not compatible and to witness the lack of respect which many dogs have for gardens it is not surprising that such a view is so often repeated.

A path has no boundaries for a dog, nor does a lawn, a rose garden, or a vegetable patch. To step from a path to a lawn via the rose bed may just be the natural process of taking the shortest route from point A to point B.

A dog can never be taught to respect a garden, or any other piece of property for that matter, but he can be made to understand which areas are forbidden and also which activities are going to produce an unpleasant response.

A dog in the garden, as in the home, will act as his instincts dictate unless these instincts are controlled and outlets are provided to satisfy his natural desires.

What then are the garden-related problems which generally affect most dog owners? Let us start with the dog who runs riot and has no garden sense whatsoever. This type of dog will be difficult to cure — he has either been allowed the full run of the garden or the previous methods of control have been quite ineffective.

The domestic control training already described in previous chapters is essential so that you can be in a position to apply verbal control to stop any undesirable activities with the follow-up of a recall whenever the need arises.

Every effort must be made to catch your dog *each* time he thinks about going on to a prohibited area. There is little value in keeping him off one patch of cultivated soil but allowing him onto another patch of similar type because you consider it to be unimportant. All cultivated ground will look the same to your dog until he has been more fully educated.

The moment you see your dog moving purposefully towards a forbidden area is the time to act. As he reaches the prohibited area, say the vegetable patch, stop him at the edge just before he steps on to it. Shout in a very positive manner '*Ben, no,*' then follow up with gentle praise; this should keep his attention from his original objective. You may then wish to recall him with great pleasure or tell him to stay whilst you walk over to give him praise. The choice is yours.

A playful dog can be taught garden sense by throwing his ball, or some other article, on to or across the prohibited area, so long as you can stop him just at the edge. A long line attached to his collar can be very effective if you have gauged the length correctly. For every throw of the ball on to or across the prohibited area he should have half a dozen chases on permitted areas to ensure that he understands that he is allowed to chase his ball but not on certain types of ground.

Many puppies are very easily educated to show respect for the garden by education from the start. Never allow your pup to follow you on to prohibited areas whilst you are weeding or carrying out other activities.

To punish a puppy or older dog for being on a prohibited area is rather late and is generally quite useless. Certainly a strong tone of voice showing your displeasure may have some effect but this should only be used to gain his attention with a more pleasant response to draw him off. This should immediately be followed by a short training session which will concentrate on getting your dog to stop at the edge of the forbidden area whilst you are in a position to control the situation.

A few garden canes and some string are often sufficient to prevent a dog from going on to prohibited areas; this type of preventive measure can easily be removed later when the dog has learnt from habit to keep off the areas in question.

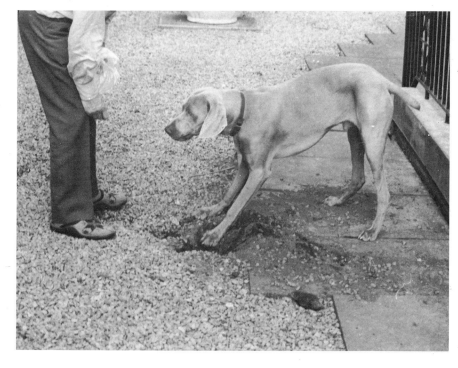

Fritz, the digger, is caught in the act.

A dog who digs is another problem and again he must be caught in the act or when he appears to be thinking about it, especially when a nicely kept lawn receives his attention. To take him back to the scene of his misdemeanour and give him a lecture or a scolding is unlikely to have any effect. If it does click in his mind he may think that the spoilt areas are taboo and will choose another spot in the same area next time, thereby infuriating his master who thinks that the dog is being disobedient.

Some dogs are incorrigible diggers and every hole they dig makes the stopping much more difficult. Remember that every time he digs in your garden he has been given the opportunity — by yourself, and you must revise your security or observation activities.

By nature the whole garden area is there for your dog's convenience and it will be used as such if his toilet activities are not controlled. If it bothers you to see his droppings in the middle of a nicely cut lawn or to find the same lawn being ruined by a multitude of burnt patches it is because you have permitted the situation to develop. Once the smell of his own waste is in the ground your dog will find it quite natural to do it there again. Garden training is certainly not as important as house training, but if specified areas are taboo then your dog must never be allowed on to these areas when he is expected to perform. Allotted areas

Kirsty views the outside world but requires no gate to keep her in.

must be set aside for his toilet purposes and he should be taken there at the appropriate times as an extension of house training. A young dog brought up in this manner will soon learn; he will make use of his designated areas and should not be a problem.

Some dogs are experts at escaping from enclosed gardens, either through fences or over gates. Their desire for freedom and the enjoyment of meeting up with other wandering canine friends can be a strong incentive to escape. However, if they had never been given the opportunity to experience this type of freedom they would not be looking for it.

Sometimes there is a natural instinct to get out and it would be too easy to blame the owners of such dogs for failing to keep their pets confined to the garden. The fence may well have been fully examined and considered escape proof but the dog has found a way. Once a dog is known to be a canine Houdini, suitable preventive measures must be taken to ensure that he does not become the terror of the neighbourhood. All likely means of exit must be blocked. A garden gate which is suitably sprung to keep it firmly shut is an advantage. A daytime kennel with a run made of strong chain-link fencing may be the answer, but to tie a dog up is seldom a satisfactory solution although it can be used as a temporary measure.

The problem of the escaping and wandering dog may be created by lack of activity — dogs who are taken out for good long walks with controlled freedom are usually quite contented when at home and do not feel any need to escape.

13 Your Dog and Children

Dogs and children seem to be such a natural combination that in most homes where both are present they certainly enjoy each other's company. However, children — like dogs — require a certain amount of adult supervision and when both get together it is most important that each learns to respect the needs of the other.

Children who play without adult supervision are governed, to a great extent, by their upbringing. There are times when situations get out of hand and youngsters in the excitement of a game, through thoughtlessness or sheer bravado, will act in a manner which may be regretted later on, especially when they are found out. Canine logic does not harbour such regrets with the same understanding as children.

The fact that so many homes containing both children and dogs are

Caro 'attacked' Sharon in the BBC drama series *The Mad Death* but really they are the best of friends.

living in complete harmony shows that they can be extremely compatible. Most homes are trouble free and this chapter has been written in the hope that it can help to prevent some of the problems which can arise and to help prevent a few of the unfortunate minority from being branded as unsuitable canine companions to children.

I have moved round the country quite a bit during the years that we have owned dogs and have witnessed the looks from neighbours as we moved into a new home together with our two or three German Shepherds (Alsatians) — it has been obvious that the undeserved reputation of this breed has affected our welcome. However, we fully understood the uneasiness of our new neighbours, appreciating their misgivings, and we always made a point of putting them at ease as soon as possible.

The children in our new neighbourhood were usually our priority. Children have a great liking for dogs unless they have had an unfortunate experience or a fearful parent who has made a point of transmitting that fear to their offspring. We found that most local children were happy to make friends with our big happy outgoing German Shepherds and we encouraged these friendships. When parents saw that their children had made these new friends and realised that these rather large canine acquaintances were well behaved and to be trusted, the dogs became fully accepted members of the community.

Unfortunately, there are homes which are quite unsuitable for a dog or homes where the introduction of a dog is doomed to disaster. There are other homes where the dog is already an integral part of the family but the introduction of a new baby has created a problem where the dog is the inevitable loser.

In most cases a puppy is brought into the family as a pet for the children and, on occasions, it is treated like a toy with little thought having been given to the pet's needs.

Although my own childhood was in a home where dogs and cats were part of the family scene, I did not accept one into my own home until I had been married for some twelve years. My sister had a labrador bitch who was due to whelp and she kept promising my two young daughters one of Birkie's puppies.

My thoughts revolved round our responsibility to the puppy as well as to our daughters. Was I prepared to see to all its requirements, feed it properly, exercise it and house train it? In those days I did not even know that dog training clubs existed. We decided to take the puppy, but only after I had decided to accept full responsibility for ensuring that it would be brought up in a satisfactory manner — a responsibility which could not be left to my ten- and four-year-old daughters.

Buying a puppy needs careful consideration, especially when the purchase is to satisfy the desires of children. Unless one parent is prepared to accept full responsibility for tending to the puppy's needs, the pet is likely to be discarded like a broken toy. Some children are quite unsuited to having a puppy about the house; they pester the dog at times when it should be sleeping (after all a young baby is taken into a separate room to sleep, away from noisy brothers or sisters — a puppy deserves the same consideration), their shrieking excited noise can be unnerving, while some children are downright cruel and will take their spite out on any form of life they consider lower than themselves.

Conversely, there are some puppies which are unsuited to the general hurly-burly of a full family life. They may be too timid to stand up to an inconsiderate family or they may be too excitable for a home where children live life to the full.

Children do get bitten by puppies and, on occasions, by more mature dogs, but more often than not the dog should not be blamed. There are many reasons why such incidents occur and the real cause is often lost in discriminating against the dog for being aggressive. Let us look at some of the basic causes.

(1) Through excitement at play where the puppy is part of a play group and in the heat of the moment the puppy has used the only faculty at his disposal — his teeth. Consider a puppy with litter brothers and sisters (this is really what children at play mean to him); puppies fight for fun, they tumble over and bite each other but never do any harm.

From my own experience, I found that if my young dog lagged behind because of something which had taken his interest and I called him in, my old bitch would run back, get behind him and nip his hind legs to let him know he should be with us. Watch young puppies and you will see that they do the same to each other; some puppies will also do this with children when they get excited and run.

Again you will see puppies take each other by the throat and shake as if it was a serious business. With the tough loose skin in that area no harm can be done, but the action dates back to canine ancestry and the fight for food where dogs went in for the kill in this manner. A young dog taking hold of a child in the same way as he bites a litter mate will normally go for the most accessible part of the body, usually the arm. This will certainly hurt and most likely break the skin but to the puppy it is just fun. To the child and his parents it is a serious matter but whose fault was it for allowing this situation to develop? — not the puppy's.

(2) Possessiveness can be a serious cause of biting and this should never be allowed to develop, because a dog who bites for this reason really means it. This will be discussed at greater depth in Chapter 15.

(3) Children can be very irritating at times and a dog may feel that respite will only be achieved by warding off the inconsiderate child with a nip or a full-blooded bite, depending on the circumstances and the dog's previous experiences. It may be the result of a long-suffering episode of

irritation — and not necessarily from the child who is bitten. If the circumstances were similar to some previous occasion a rather innocent child may receive the bite — a result of previous actions by another child.

(4) Some dogs, but fortunately very few, appear to be naturally bad-tempered. They may, however, be in pain and a pat in the wrong place from an unsuspecting child may well result in an automatic reaction of warning the culprit off. Again these indications of aggression are dealt with in Chapter 15.

(5) Jealousy can be another cause of canine problems, especially when the first baby arrives in a home. A young dog is likely to accept the baby as a welcome addition to the family, but the older dog who has received all the affection of a childless home is likely to object if that affection is cut off and transferred to the new arrival. The dog may, therefore, consider the baby to be a rival and could act in a manner foreign to his former character.

The arrival of a baby into a sensible home where the dog continues to receive attention as well as affection and is encouraged to accept the baby, will usually result in a contented dog who is happy to accept an added responsibility — that of looking after the new member of the family.

It must also be remembered that a dog belonging to grandparents and accustomed to their exclusive attention, is likely to object to the visit of a new grandchild if the pet is made to feel cut off from his customary pampering during these family visits.

The foregoing paragraphs, I think, bring out the main causes why children are bitten by dogs and, although some children must accept the responsibility for the dog's reaction, it is the duty of the parents and dog owners to educate and control both child and dog to ensure that both grow up with the appropriate measure of respect for each other.

We read in the press from time to time about incidents of grief where children have been badly bitten by dogs, but there are many more instances of dogs showing an uncanny understanding for young children.

We sold one of our German Shepherd puppies to a couple with very young twins; they told us of an occasion when the puppy was about ten months old and the twins were just toddling. Mum was upstairs attending to the household chores when she heard the puppy whimpering. She came downstairs to investigate the cause and found one of the twins chewing the puppy's ear and the puppy lying there putting up with the irritation and inconvenience.

My three-year-old grandson was playing in the garden one day with the family's four-month-old German Shepherd puppy, when he ran into the house crying and holding his arm. Before his Mum had a chance to ask what had happened, the little fellow burst out with 'Don't tell me "I told you so".' He had obviously been playing rough and the puppy had responded in a similar manner. My grandson has grown to have more respect for his canine companion, the dog has developed a higher level of tolerance and the two are the best of friends.

Another dog, a much more mature Cocker Spaniel, belonged to neighbours, a childless young couple. She was very affectionate but decidedly bad-tempered about anything which did not suit her. If she was in possession of a bone a growl would be sufficient to ward off her owners; trying to examine her ears or feet would result in a similar response. This little dog was in full control.

This was a very undesirable situation which should not have been tolerated and the pending arrival of a new baby worried the owners very much. There were thoughts of finding a new home for the dog but a natural reluctance to part with her resulted in a lack of positive action.

A baby girl duly arrived, the dog stayed and to everyone's surprise the dog's reaction was one of total attentive affection to the baby. As the baby grew into a toddler, this bad-tempered animal accepted the child near her bone and at her food dish; the dog also accepted the pulling at her ears and feet — that toddler could do no wrong but the parents still received the warning growl if they stepped out of line.

Children love to take dogs out for a walk and there is nothing better than seeing a youngster with his (or her) dog enjoying each other's company. The freedom of the open spaces, of woods or parkland is there to be enjoyed so long as the youngster has the control and sense of responsibility to ensure that his canine companion will respect his young master's authority.

Kerry takes Mac for his walk after school.

14 Your Dog and the Vet

The services of a vet are just as important to our canine companions as the services of a doctor are to ourselves. Some dog owners are fortunate enough to have minimal requirements for such a service, whilst others seem to be the principal contributors to the income of a veterinary practice.

Whatever the medical requirements of our dogs during their lives, proper attention from the vet can only be given if the 'patient' is prepared to cooperate and permit a proper physical examination.

One must be very sympathetic to the problems that vets have to face with dogs who squirm and refuse to be handled or snap or bite as soon as a strange hand approaches them. Muzzling such dogs may be the answer but this can only make the situation worse on future such ocasions — the dog will carry vivid memories of the unpleasant muzzling during previous veterinary visits.

Why are so many dogs such a problem when they visit the vet's surgery and what can be done to minimise these problems? I would think that the causes can be associated with the following reasons.

(a) Past experiences at the surgery. A puppy could have had an unfortunate encounter in the waiting room, or the claustrophobic atmosphere of such a place with so many people and their dogs could well have a very strong and undesirable impression on a youngster. Also the encounter with the vet himself may well have been a harrowing experience. To be manhandled and possibly injected, even by a gentle and considerate vet, could be the final indignity after a rather unpleasant period in the waiting room. A dog's first visit to the vet can leave a lasting impression which may never be fully erased.

(b) The temperament of the dog may well be such that nobody but the family can approach him, and the forced attentions of a vet could leave a dog with a lasting impression of unpleasantness.

(c) The dog may be spoilt and out of control, with the owner completely at the mercy of his dog's desires. A dog with a wilful disposition which has been allowed to develop and gather strength will certainly be more than a match for his owner and will give the vet a very trying time.

To prevent or overcome the various problems one must consider the original cause and how to counter the situation.

(a) A puppy's first visit to the vet's surgery should be completely devoid of unpleasantness and it is certainly advisable to avoid a crowded waiting room. It may be possible to time the visit for when the surgery is quiet; if not, one member of the family can book the puppy in to wait his turn whilst another sits in the car with the youngster. The person in the waiting room then comes out to collect the puppy when his turn comes to receive attention. This first visit might be arranged purely to have your puppy meet the vet, without any unpleasant injections to give your pet a disagreeable impression of the person who should be his friend.

The smell of disinfectant may well trigger off unpleasant memories of a previous visit to the surgery and it could be helpful to have your dog accustomed to the smell of the particular disinfectant used by your vet. A little on your hands from time to time can get him used to the smell, especially under very pleasant conditions. At feeding time or whilst you are having fun and games, would be suitable. You can also have friends handle and fondle your dog whilst the smell of disinfectant is in the vicinity; this will help him to cope with situations he will meet in the surgery.

(b) Dogs of a shy or retiring nature will show this failing at any time in a strange situation but a visit to the vet's surgery where unpleasantness cannot be readily avoided can only make the situation worse. It is, therefore, the responsibility of the owners of such dogs to take all steps necessary to overcome this problem outside the confines of the vet's surgery.

To shelter such a dog from situations which are considered to be unpleasant will not cure the problem, neither will the forcing of disagreeable situations bring forth a cure.

The foundation of a happier and more relaxed relationship can be attained by attending a local breed or obedience club where people with sympathy, understanding and knowledge of this type of problem can give personal assistance in dispelling the dog's fears.

(c) Owners of dogs who are out of control and who have a wilful disposition certainly require to take their dogs in hand and should be applying the principles and training procedures already described in this book — especially the training to achieve the requirements of stay training in Chapter 8.

All dogs should be trained to accept handling by all members of the family and also by strangers. It is remarkable just how many dogs will not stand to be examined by their closest human companions.

Your dog should be happy to stand whilst he is being physically examined (or groomed), to have your hands feel through his coat, to feel his bone structure, down over his shoulders, over his back and along his ribs, over his hindquarters and down his hind legs.

Whilst he is sitting he should be happy to let you examine his teeth, to clear any dirt away from the corners of his eyes and to examine and clean his ears.

Whilst he is lying down he should let you examine and, if need be, clean his undercarriage, also to examine his feet at length. Cut pads are quite a common occurrence these days and are very difficult to attend to if your dog is not very cooperative.

If your dog is sufficiently experienced through your own efforts to carry out such examinations, his cooperative attitude is likely to extend to the vet's surgery. You will gain your vet's appreciation and your dog's peace of mind at a time when he needs to be relaxed and willing to co-operate.

This Boxer should be a pleasure for the vet to examine.

Examining your dog's teeth should be a regular occurrence, but it can only be carried out if your dog is under control.

Assi having her feet examined.

15 Barking and Aggressive Dogs

Barking dogs

Dogs who bark at their pleasure are certainly a nuisance to their owners and their neighbours, but the barking dog also has his value as a warning and a deterrent.

Even the smallest dogs with an irritating bark have great value. I remember my mother's Miniature Dachsie, Mark, and how effective he was as a watch dog. My mother had left her key with a neighbour so that a workman could be let into the house to carry out some repairs. When the workman and the neighbour walked up the path to the door, little Mark barked his head off in a manner which let the 'intruders' know that they were not welcome. The workman refused to go into the house even with the neighbour.

It will, therefore, be seen that any attempt to stop a dog from barking should take into consideration the value of his guarding instinct and the desire to keep it alive. This is a good reason why suitable training should be given to control barking so that effective commands can be given to start and stop your dog barking at your pleasure.

There are a variety of reasons why a dog will bark but these can generally be grouped into three categories.

(a) The guarding or protective instinct.
(b) To gain attention; the dog who is shut in the house whilst the owner goes out, is left in the kennel or is left out in the garden.
(c) The dog who barks through over-excitement.

Whatever the reason for your dog barking, you should start to control the situation by teaching him to speak and then be quiet on command. This approach will prevent the inhibitions which would otherwise affect his guarding or protective instincts and will act as a safety valve by creating an outlet for the natural desire to bark. No dog can have his strong barking instinct completely suppressed without losing some of his natural character.

The procedure of teaching your dog to speak on command is to praise him whenever he barks of his own volition. The reason for his barking is unimportant, just encourage him with 'That's a good boy, Ben, *speak*,' and repeat as you wish, but five seconds of barking is long enough then stop him.

Make your directive to stop barking very clear and as loud as you wish — your bark can be louder and more meaningful than his. '*Ben, enough,*' is all that is required and is repeated as necessary with appropriate physical gestures to enforce your point. You should then give your dog praise for his silence with 'That's a good boy, that's enough,' given in a suitable tone of voice.

Five seconds of canine silence should then be followed by further encouragement to bark and induced by 'Speak, Ben, that's a good boy, speak.' A repeat of five seconds barking is quite sufficient to serve your purpose with a follow-up command for silence with sufficient forcefulness to achieve your objective.

When you can get your dog to bark at your request and follow up with silence as soon as you demand it, you have created a situation of total control which can then be extended to the various natural situations which cause annoyance.

It is now possible to select the situations where barking is completely forbidden. The dog who barks because he is left behind can be told to shut up in no uncertain manner as soon as he starts barking. The same with dogs who chase back and forth behind the garden fence when somebody is walking past.

The dog who barks when somebody comes in the garden gate or knocks at the front door should still be encouraged for a few seconds before being told that enough is enough.

You, the owner, must be the master of the particular situation. It may not be possible to prevent your dog from barking but, at least, you should be able to control the situation.

Aggressive dogs

Aggression is quite another matter and must be taken very seriously. There are occasions when serious aggression can be justified but, in a domestic environment, these situations are very few and far between.

Fortunately most dogs, either through their breeding, upbringing or both, are docile and friendly in character and this makes them ideal pets. However, we find from time to time that things do go wrong; breeding from overprotective dogs can result in the offspring getting into the hands of people who do not appreciate the nature of the dogs they have taken on. Breeding from nervous dogs can also create problems and the lack of ability on the part of some owners to control such dogs can bring out certain canine traits which would otherwise have remained dormant.

There are a variety of reasons why a dog shows aggressive tendencies and these can come to the surface in quite a number of different ways. To understand canine aggression it should be recognised that in most cases this characteristic is purely a defensive reaction. It may well be that the dog who attacks without any apparent reason is probably applying the old maxim 'The best form of defence is to attack,' and we should consider any sign or threat of aggression to be a situation where the dog feels it to be in his best interests to attack, or at least to give warning that to encroach on his territory any further would result in attack.

Few dogs go beyond the warning stage of a growl, or a baring of teeth or a meaningful bark, but this is because the transgressor withdraws. The latter may well be the dog's owner who wishes to sit on his own easy chair but the dog has already taken up residence, has claimed full squatter's rights and has obviously got away with it on previous occasions.

If we accept that canine aggression, or the threat of it, is a defensive reaction we can now look at some of the reasons why a dog should feel it necessary to defend.

Self-preservation is often the reaction of a dog who is cornered or feels that he cannot get away from a situation which he cannot face. A dog on a lead and in the company of his owner may feel that he is cornered; the situation may seem to be quite normal to us but a timid dog or a dog who has not been adequately socialised can visualise all sorts of possibilities when a stranger approaches, or if he receives the attentions of another dog. He could well have tried to back away in the past and found that the restriction of the lead made him feel vulnerable so he has decided that to defend himself he must attack, or at least put on a show of strength to dissuade this imaginary aggressor that he means business.

A very self-assured dog can also become aggressive as a means of protecting his own sense of superiority. A very dominant dog or bitch will show superiority by taking a very dominant stance. This type of dog may not even growl or bare his teeth but a canine adversary will know from that stance that it is a warning sign that must be heeded.

It is worth noting at this stage that a male dog will very rarely attack a bitch, although a bitch will attack a dog for the same reason that a young lady will spurn the advances of a persistent human stud. However, the canine male will normally accept such a warning and refuse to fight. Two male dogs together can be a different story, especially if one feels that the honour of his female companion is in danger. I am often aware of the latter situation when I take my own two German Shepherds out for a walk. My male dog will fix his eye on any other male who comes near my young bitch and he has to be firmly controlled to ensure that he does not chase this adversary off his patch.

Two bitches together are also liable to fight if their characters are too evenly balanced. In cases like this, one bitch feels it necessary to dominate the other; it may be a fit of jealousy or possessiveness which sparks off the trouble, but if the more submissive bitch refuses to give way to the attacker a fight will ensue. Fights of this nature can be the most vicious and damaging of all, and any signs of bad feeling between two bitches should not be ignored but be taken as a warning of the events which could follow.

It is extremely unlikely that an adult dog of either sex will make a serious attack on a puppy. He may well show a great pretence of aggression by growling or baring of teeth and may even appear to make a vicious attack if provoked by a cheeky puppy, but the seriousness of the attack will stop short of a damaging bite.

On one occasion, a young dog, a Cocker Spaniel of about a year old, ventured in through my garage whilst I was working on my car. I had not seen the dog go past me and he walked undetected through the garage, the garden and straight into the house through the open back door. Caro, my German Shepherd, was lying in the lounge at my wife's feet when this little stranger presented himself in front of Caro's nose.

The first I knew of the confrontation was the noise in the garden and the Spaniel trapped in a corner. He was on his back with Caro on top, his jaws full of Spaniel neck. The noise was one of terror with the little dog crying for mercy. I shouted to Caro to let go which he did immediately. The owners of the Spaniel were by now at hand to retrieve their dog, who amazingly did not have a mark on him and was none the worse for the experience.

It was obvious that Caro's action was that of a warning rather than a determined attack on the unwanted intruder. Caro could not be blamed for taking steps to protect his home against an uninvited visitor. I could be criticised for leaving the garage doors open, providing a means of entry to the garden, but the full responsibility lay with the owners of the Spaniel for allowing their dog the freedom to enter private property. They were walking this young dog without a lead.

The foregoing episode brings out a few interesting and important points relating to canine reactions and human responsibilities.

Protecting his own property is a natural trait in a dog and the story of Caro's encounter with the Spaniel gives a very good insight into a dog's attitude towards such territorial protection. Some dogs have a very strong protective instinct and this must be controlled; to be warned by your dog that somebody is opening the garden gate or knocking at the door should certainly be encouraged, but that should be the limit of your dog's protective duties.

Some dogs exhibit a desire to protect their owners and may act in a rather unsociable manner under normal conditions. Unfortunately these reactions are often the result of the owner's attitude. He may be of a nervous disposition and his dog reacts by feeling that he should protect his master at all times. A puppy may have taken an objection to meeting a stranger whilst out for a walk with his owner, who thought this to be

Corrie is giving his
attention to a visitor
who would be unwise to
open the gate.

rather clever and encouraged his puppy instead of showing his disapproval. In due course, this protective instinct has gathered strength
and the owner does not know how to counter the situation. Some dogs,
however, become overprotective whilst they are growing up through the
period of adolescence. This is a natural process in some cases, but if not
curbed from the start such unsociable reactions can become a way of life.

The covetous dog is the one who lays claim to certain items of property
and dares all to encroach on his self-claimed territory. He growls, he
bares his teeth or he may even bite his owner as he guards his possessions.
This is the biggest problem which any owner has to face.

When a dog takes possession of his owner's chair and refuses to give it
up, when he stands growling over a bone or his dinner dish as his owner
or someone else passes by, when these situations have become a way of
life the owner has abdicated his authority and responsibility and has
accepted that his dog has become the senior and most dominant member
of their small community.

Cases like this develop from a lack of understanding or weakness on
the part of the owner. Puppies will always defend their property against
the attentions of their litter mates until the pecking order has been sorted

out and firmly established. In this way, each puppy finds its own place; this is a development of nature and a great number of these puppies will apply the same principles when they go into a new home.

Unfortunately a number of puppy owners think it is rather clever to see their young pet guarding his bone or dinner dish. Each time this occurs and as the puppy matures into an adult, his confidence grows and he is eventually allowed to assume full control over any situation which takes his fancy. Under these circumstances the owners are frightened of the little, or big, monsters they have unconsciously cultivated and to reverse the roles of dominance they must take positive steps to regain their rightful function as masters over their possessive pet. Prevention or cure is based on the need for the owner to show that he can master his dog's aggressive outlook. By that I mean aggression must be countered by aggression, tempered to suit the occasion, without resentfulness and without malice, but it must be administered in a manner which the dog understands.

To counter any canine aggressive tendencies you must be in a position to enforce your will; if you can succeed by voice alone and at a distance so much the better, but success can only be measured by a positive response on the *first* command. This can make life so much easier for yourself and your dog. Generally however, a more forceful approach is required, to be carried out in situations where your dog cannot escape from your actions.

Hitting your dog is out, either by hand or with a rolled-up newspaper; a dog will soon learn to dodge this and may retaliate if he feels so inclined.

Situations should be anticipated and you should have your dog on a lead at the time when corrective action is required. Corrective action must be short and sharp to achieve the response you require and his neck is your target. Remember Caro's deterrent with the Cocker Spaniel.

There are two variations of a general approach which can be applied and they are as follows.

(a) Take hold of the loose skin at your dog's neck, two handfuls if you like, look him straight in the eye and tell him what you think of him (just as a bitch will put a delinquent youngster in his place): '*No, Ben, that is quite enough*,' is all that is required, and it can be repeated. Three seconds of this treatment should be quite sufficient. Let him go and then tell him how good he is. Get his attention firmly fixed on yourself and away from the source of trouble.

(b) This approach is similar to (a) but on this occasion put your left hand in between his slip collar and his neck. Pull tight on the lead with your right hand and twist the collar with your left. Your knuckles will dig into his neck muscles and it will be very unpleasant for him. Again you must give a very strong verbal reprimand until you release your grip when it is all praise and pleasantness. Three seconds of pressure on his neck is long enough — remember that you are choking your dog — but aggression must be countered effectively by aggression. As with (a) get his attention away from the trouble source and on yourself as you release him.

These methods must, of course, be applied with the measure of force required to achieve a satisfactory response and, with faults of long standing, they will probably require to be repeated on a number of occasions. I must also emphasise that these measures must not be carried out in a temper or with malice. They are designed to be unpleasant and only your aggression — deliberate, but controlled — will cure the problem which *must be stamped out.* Many a dog has finished up as the subject of a court case because the owner failed to appreciate the effects of his own weaknesses.

We will now look at the various problems which have already been reviewed and consider prevention and cure.

The very first signs of aggression must be countered immediately; the barking of a puppy or older dog at someone coming to the house is permissible and to be encouraged as already described, but the action of a puppy or adult who bares his teeth under these circumstances is not to be tolerated. However, the puppy or dog who barks whilst out on the lead because of an approaching dog or human must be stopped immediately, unless the circumstances are very suspicious.

The timid dog who acts aggressively must be treated in the same manner as the dominant dog who wishes to show his superiority. He must be dominated with the neck treatment as described above, but he should immediately be removed from the source of the trouble when praise, love and affection can be given to counter a very unpleasant situation.

If circumstances permit an immediate return to the scene of the trouble, you should take advantage of the situation to assess your dog's reaction. He may require some pleasant backing from yourself to help him regain confidence but any sign of a return to his aggressive behaviour will again require the neck treatment to let him know that you disapprove very strongly. Take him away from the scene and again give him praise and affection.

To show your displeasure twice in such a short period is usually quite enough and you should try to avoid any further undesirable situations that day. A build-up of unpleasant situations should always be avoided as this is going to affect the relationship between yourself and your dog. It can also affect your own actions and irrational thinking can replace your previously controlled approach to the problem.

One common mistake which is made by many dog owners is in their attitude towards canine wanderers that they meet up with whilst out for a walk with their own dogs. When another dog comes over to investigate their own pet most owners will shout and threaten the stranger, even throwing stones or trying to chase it away. This aggressive human attitude only serves to bring out aggressiveness in their own dog. Any threatening attitude on the part of a dog owner can only make his dog feel more powerful and keen to support his master; alternatively, a timid dog may become more frightened and may want to attack the source of his fear — the other dog.

The dog owner now has a dual problem: (1) controlling his own dog and (2) trying to get rid of the unwanted visitor. It is of course advisable to be more observant in the first place and to avoid loose dogs where possible. However, this is not always feasible and there are occasions when it is extremely difficult to ward off a strange dog without bringing out the aggressiveness in your own pet.

My own approach (as described earlier) when I am caught in such a situation is to hold my own dog close and turn round in a manner which gives me the opportunity to give the other dog a back heel kick whilst I am speaking nicely to my own dog, who does not realise that I have taken positive and aggressive action. The hit or near miss on the other dog's chin normally sends him packing.

The dog who protects his 'own' property against his owner is obviously creating a disastrous situation and this should be stopped at the very first instance. A very sharp 'No' and physically making your dog comply with your requirements will kill off any thoughts of repetition of the offence. If your dog has appropriated your chair and does not want to get off he should be put off immediately and your feelings made very clear — but again, this must be without temper or malice and should be followed by a few words of praise. Remember that praise is not a sign of weakness but is a recognition by you of his acceptance of your action.

If your dog growls when he has food a very positive and commanding 'No' is essential, then take his food away from him. Again tell him how good he is, then give his food back to him. Walk away from your dog, then return and pick up his food dish again to test his reaction. If your dog persists with his possessiveness and an aggressive attitude then you must give him the neck treatment and also take the food away again, immediately returning it to him with plenty of praise.

Do not avoid the problem or give your dog the opportunity to challenge your authority but cut him down to size if he tries to become the dominant partner.

For the dog who is already in command of the situation and if you have a real fear of being bitten, put his lead on or attach a long line to his slip collar prior to feeding time or if you are giving him a bone. Set up a situation which will be under your full control.

Whenever somebody goes close enough and receives a threatening response from the dog give your pet a hefty jerk on the lead or line along with a vocal blasting, then call him in to you for praise and affection. Let him go back or take him back to the food and repeat the process as necessary until you are satisfied with his response.

It may take a long time before you feel safe to pick up his bone or food dish whilst it is in his possession, but at the very least you should demand that your dog will leave it and come back to you on command.

The dog who settles into your easy chair or on the bed can be treated in the same way — with the lead or long line. Another approach, however, is to put inflated balloons on the forbidden resting place. If these are tied in a manner which will keep them in place it will only require one loudly bursting balloon to deter him from returning to that particular spot.

This has been a chapter of unpleasantness for both dog and owner, but by facing up to the realities of the situation the owner is accepting his responsibilities and duty to his canine companion as well as to society by making the change to a life of true companionship.

16 Kennels — Outdoors or Indoors

Generally, the domestic dog spends his life with his owner's house as one large indoor kennel and is quite happy with a bed in a corner somewhere. Many have no special bed at all, having — with certain restrictions — their own selected areas for rest or sleep.

However, many of the problems which have already been discussed — especially those related to destructive tendencies, the garden escapist and the over-protective dog — can be relieved for convenient periods by the use of a permanent outdoor kennel or a movable pet pen, although problems are unlikely to be cured by restricting a dog in such a manner.

A kennel with an outside run and placed in a suitable corner of the garden can give a dog (or dogs) periods of peaceful existence away from the activity of a busy household or it can give an owner some respite to get on with household chores without having to keep a watchful eye on a mischievous canine companion. Although my own dogs are house pets they willingly spend three to four hours most mornings in their kennel or

A good sturdy kennel and run.

run. They also go out again at our bedtime until we get up in the morning.

The positioning of a kennel is very important. From the two photographs it will be seen that one is in a secluded, quiet corner of the garden with a large bush giving shelter from the sun. The fencing and garage wall create protection from the wind, especially on a cold winter's night. The other kennel has been nicely converted from a garden shed, and has a good concrete run with a stout fence. The dogs lie at the other side of this kennel for shade when the sun is at its height. Unfortunately, the latter kennel is not ideally sited. One side of the run is adjacent to a yard behind some shops and the other side adjoins a lane. The activity from children, and grown men with minds like little boys, who love to tease a dog through a fence can cause temperament problems when the dog in question meets the relevant age groups in the street.

It will, therefore, be seen that when siting a kennel full consideration must be given to the possibility of outside interference, protection from the weather and any other factor which may affect the suitability of your choice.

A secluded kennel and run.

Pet pens are now becoming more extensively recognised for their value in the home and can, in certain circumstances, be considered as an alternative to an outdoor kennel. They have been popular among breed exhibitors for quite some time, especially for the transportation of the smaller breeds. They are also very useful for keeping valuable show specimens out of harm's way when they are not in the show ring.

Within the domestic environment problems can be resolved or prevented by the use of these pet pens — especially when the canine companion has destructive tendencies. A few hours' absence on a shopping expedition or an evening out can result in damage beyond belief when boredom or the teething stage of a puppy's growth has led the family pet into acts which are considered by the human mind to be pure vandalism.

The size of the pet pen must be adequate for the breed of dog.

Pet pens may be considered to be expensive, especially the sizes required for larger dogs. However, the cost of a pen is usually small when related to the value of articles rendered useless by the destructive pet. A bonus comes from an easy mind and the elimination of an unhappy homecoming which often results in a loss of temper and another canine beating which usually proves to be quite useless.

The pen also makes ideal sleeping quarters at night and prevents early morning wanderings and destructive forays into probibited areas. This use can be extended to cover daytime rest periods, possibly with the door left open so that the dog can come and go as it wishes.

Travelling can be made so much easier with a pet pen. The dog's containment will assist the driver's concentration, and prevent damage to the interior of the car if the pet is left for any length of time.

Getting a youngster or older dog accustomed to a pet pen, however, is very important and its abuse as a convenient method of getting a dog unnecessarily out of the way can be classed as mental cruelty. Your first objective is to have your dog willing to enter the pen and to be content to stay there. The time to do this is when he is tired and ready for his bed. Put his bed into the pen along with a juicy bone, a biscuit, or a play toy and induce him into it. Alternatively, his main meal of the day can be put into the pen so that he can feed and feel free to come out when finished. A few days of this before using the pen for its intended purpose can help to create a relaxed atmosphere without your dog feeling caged.

With his meal in one corner and his bed taking up the remainder of the floor space it should not be difficult to shut your dog in for short, then extended, periods of time until he is completely at home. To have the pen by your fireside chair whilst you are reading a book or watching television can also help to create a settled atmosphere and may well pay handsome dividends. It is important to build up his confidence and relaxation in his new quarters. Any pampering is likely to delay the acceptance of this new environment.

Pet pens must be used with discretion and should not take away the purpose of having a dog — that of companionship. Periods of solitude can be of value to both owner and dog and make for a happier companionship. However, canine loneliness resulting from long periods of isolation, be it caged beside you or kennelled at the bottom of the garden, brings out the question — why keep a dog?

When there is more than one animal in the house, care must be taken to ensure that the dog in question does not feel caged whilst the others are free. This can result in jealousies which may well develop into rivalries and the inevitable fights where no animal is the real winner and the owner must always be the loser.

17 A Code of Good Manners

This book has been written to help you to understand, train and enjoy your canine friend. His companionship was the reason for taking on the responsibility of a dog, but this should not detract from your responsibility to the community. A pet dog must fit into the community as a creature of pleasure and not a social burden to the neighbourhood.

When I was writing my first book *Training the Alsatian* (now reprinted as *Training the German Shepherd*) I was rather conscious of the undeserved reputation which rested on the shoulders of this magnificent breed and to help owners project a more appropriate image of their dogs I set out a Code of Good Manners.

In a slightly modified form this code is now presented to every dog owner who attends my training classes and I make no apology for including it here.

(1) Some people love dogs and others hate them. There is no need to try and convert the dog lovers but respect for the views of the others can only help to convert them in the long term.

(2) A dog should *never* be out on the street on his own. The temptation to investigate the outside world and become one of a pack can be very great. The stray dog is gun fodder for the dog haters.

(3) Keep your dog on the lead until you reach a suitable exercise area. There is nothing clever about taking a dog for a walk without a lead. Another loose dog may cause a fight, a cat may cause him to dart on to the road. It only requires a passing motor car and the prospect of human and canine tragedy is very real.

(4) When your dog is free in an exercise area keep an eye on him, especially if another dog comes into view; the other dog could be a fighter.

(5) Do not let your dog soil the pavement or a public place. Give him the opportunity at the right time and in the right place and there will be little chance of an accident.

(6) A walk on the lead should not be a constant battle between dog and owner, with the dog constantly trying to pull his owner's arm out of its

socket. The first training element of the recall exercise should be very helpful in gaining the correct measure of control.

(7) Your dog must respond to the recall when instructed; this is essential.

(8) Your dog should be taught to go down immediately where and when instructed. In an emergency this may be more necessary than the recall.

(9) Your dog should always be prepared to accept a reasonable measure of control and when young children or elderly people are around it may be advisable to keep him on a lead. A boisterous dog can so easily knock down the very young or the elderly. Children can thus become frightened of dogs for life while the elderly are very prone to injury.

(10) Rough games with a dog can be enjoyable, but can be a dangerous form of amusement if the dog is not under sufficient control to stop when required.

(11) Do not let your dog become overprotective, either of yourself or of his food. He should be quite prepared to accept strangers, although he does not have to welcome them. He should never be permitted to show signs of aggression when he is eating.

(12) Do not tolerate unnecessary barking. If your dog is telling you that somebody is approaching, tell him how good he is then distract him from the cause. If the barking continues then forceful action is required.

(13) Do not let your dog jump up to welcome people. If you and your friends get down to his level when he comes to welcome you the habit of jumping up can be avoided.

(14) Do not let your dog jump out of the car in an uncontrolled manner. It is preferable to train him to wait until after the door has been opened, then call him out when you are ready. This may well prevent an accident.

(15) Always be on the lookout for faults developing. An amusing situation with a puppy can develop into a very serious problem as he matures.

(16) Respect the farmer's land and livestock. You may know that your dog will not cause problems but there is no need to worry the farmer.

Index